CASSIDY

CHRISTIAN ROMANTIC SUSPENSE

OATH OF HONOR

LAURA SCOTT

CHAPTER ONE

Snowflakes melted on his face. Blinking in confusion, he wondered why in the world he was outside lying on the cold, hard ground.

Pushing himself into a sitting position, he winced when his head throbbed with pain. He lifted his hand and found the source, a large bump and a gash of broken skin on the back of his head. When he saw the blood on his fingers, he grimaced and cleaned them with the freshly fallen snow.

He was in danger. The primitive instinct to get away couldn't be ignored. But as he gazed around, he didn't see a car or any other source of transportation.

Had he walked there? Or been dumped like garbage?

A sense of urgency hit hard. He needed to get far away before whoever had hit him returned. His thoughts were muddled; he couldn't remember what had happened. How he'd gotten there. Or why he was even there. Yet a single thought flashed through his mind.

Cassidy. He desperately needed to find Cassidy.

The image of a beautiful redhead was the only clear memory that came to the forefront of his mind. Somehow, he managed to get to his feet. His sneakered feet slipped in the snow, and he frowned when he realized his feet were wet and cold.

His hands too. He patted his coat pockets but didn't find gloves. Or a phone. He checked his back jeans pocket and shouldn't have been surprised to find his wallet was gone.

Had he been robbed?

Where exactly was he? Why was he there? And how long had he been unconscious?

Stepping carefully, he made his way down the slippery and deserted stretch of road. He scanned his surroundings. Something about the area was vaguely familiar. Not that he remembered ever having been there before, but because of the open space where some construction work appeared to have been done. Hadn't he overheard someone talking about a deserted building along an isolated stretch of road? The memory hung like mist in the air, just out of reach.

Why couldn't he remember?

The lights whizzing by made him realize he wasn't far from the interstate. Yet seeing cars wasn't exactly reassuring. What if the person who assaulted and robbed him returned?

A sense of panic hit hard. How would he manage to find Cassidy?

He stumbled but managed to stay upright. Nausea swirled in his belly, and the pain in his head grew worse with every step. Still, he kept moving, placing one foot in front of the other toward the highway that seemed impossibly far away.

As he grew closer, it was clear the road he was on crossed over the highway. A gas station sign gave him hope.

He had to believe whoever was manning the gas station would allow him to borrow a phone.

Headlights from a car illuminated the road up ahead, and he instinctively ducked and darted into the clump of trees. His heart thundered in his chest as bitter fear coated his tongue. Were the bad guys coming back to finish him off?

Crouching down behind the bare trees, he watched as the vehicle rolled past. Maybe it was his imagination, but he thought the car moved slower than the weather conditions dictated.

A cautious driver? Maybe.

Yet once the car disappeared from his line of sight, he didn't move. Didn't head back out toward the gas station. He didn't trust anyone.

Except Cassidy.

But she wasn't there. He forced himself to stay where he was, despite the cold winter wind. When he began to shiver, he realized he was being foolish. There was no reason to risk hypothermia.

Leaving the relative shelter of the trees, he quickened his pace, lightly jogging to get the blood flowing through his veins. The motion made his head hurt, but he did his best to ignore the discomfort.

At this point, pain meant he was alive.

And he fully intended to stay that way.

He finally reached the gas station, thrilled beyond reason to see it included a small store. A bell jingled when he walked in, and he stood for a moment, savoring the warmth.

A dark-skinned man behind the counter eyed him suspiciously. He tried to smile, but his face felt frozen.

Maybe he had frostbite. He wasn't an expert on that sort of thing.

What was his expertise? Again, there was nothing but swirling mist where his memories should have been.

"May I help you?" The clerk's tone was clipped as if he wasn't happy to have him as a customer.

He pulled his hands from his pockets, lifting them up in a gesture meant to reassure the clerk he meant no harm. "I'm sorry, but I've been robbed. I don't have my wallet or my phone. I was hoping I could borrow your phone to make a call."

"No phone," the clerk said. The way the guy's hand hovered under the desk out of sight made him worried he had a gun back there.

"Okay, look, I understand. You don't know me and don't trust me. But I can't walk all the way to . . ." He hesitated. Where did Cassidy live? Greenland? He didn't remember, but he did have a phone number in his head. At least, he hoped the number belonged to her. The way his brain was working, the number might have belonged to Mickey Mouse. "Would you please make a call for me? I need a friend to pick me up."

"Fine." The man scowled as if the simple task was a huge imposition. "What's the number?"

After a brief hesitation, he recited the digits. Why the phone number and Cassidy's face were the only clear images in his mind, he had no idea. But he was grateful the clerk had agreed to make the call.

He moved away from the door, grateful for the meager warmth. He eyed the snacks but wasn't hungry.

"No answer." The clerk waved his hand. "You go now."

He didn't move, trying to figure out what to do. Call the police? For some reason, he didn't want to go that route.

He and the clerk jumped when the phone rang. With reluctance, the clerk answered. "Hello? Yes, just one moment." The clerk scowled as he slid the phone under the glass window separating them.

He grabbed the phone and lifted it to his ear. "Cassidy? Is that you?"

"Who is this?" a familiar female voice asked.

"I—uh." He frowned, wondering why his name didn't pop into his mind. "I need a ride. I've been robbed and need a ride."

"Gabe? Is that you? You've really been robbed?"

"Yes. I don't have my phone or my wallet." A sense of calm washed over him. The name Gabe sounded right. Although it seemed strange not to know his own name. "I'm sorry, but I need a ride."

"Okay, where are you calling from?"

"From a gas station. Um, what's the address?" he asked the clerk. When he rattled it off, Gabe repeated it for Cassidy.

"I know that area. I'll be there as quickly as possible. Are you sure you're okay?"

No, he wasn't okay. But of course, he answered, "Yes. I'll be fine. Just get here soon."

"I'm on my way." Cassidy disconnected from the call.

Dazed and relieved, he slid the device under the glass. "Thank you. My friend Cassidy will be here soon."

The clerk nodded, his expression indicating Gabe was welcome to stay inside to wait.

He lifted his hand to the back of his head again. What had happened? A simple robbery?

Or something more sinister?

For some strange reason, he felt certain there was nothing simple about what had happened to him.

Danger lurked nearby. Too bad he couldn't remember anything about who might have come after him or why.

———

TACTICAL POLICE OFFICER Cassidy Sommer quickly dressed and headed out to the garage attached to her condo. Why on earth was Gabe way out near the Wildflower Motel? Had he met someone there and been robbed?

She didn't want to believe the team's tech guru would do something illegal, but she was at a loss as to why he was so far away, considering he lived closer to the lakefront in White Gull Bay. Upon reaching the interstate, she hit the gas, speeding as fast as she dared. The hour wasn't that late, only ten thirty at night, which meant traffic wasn't a problem. Hopefully, she wouldn't be pulled over by the state patrol.

It was difficult to imagine a legitimate reason for Gabe so far outside the city. She considered Gabe to be a good friend; she felt certain she'd have known if he'd done something illegal. Besides, Gabe worked for the Milwaukee Police Department. As a civilian, yes, but he still needed to keep his record clean.

Soft snowflakes melted when they hit her windshield, and the outside temperature hovered at 32 degrees. Christmas, her favorite holiday, was only three weeks away, and she was planning a party for the entire tactical team for the weekend before the actual holiday since she knew her teammates would want to spend that time with their families. Joe Kingsley and Elly in particular were expecting their first baby on the day after Christmas.

All her teammates were getting married or engaged. She was still the odd one out but tried not to focus on that. She had been engaged once, but the guy who'd claimed to love her abruptly decided he didn't want to be married to a cop. Last she'd heard, Wade Morris was happily married to an accountant.

Goody for him, she thought with a sigh. Obviously, he hadn't loved her as much as she had cared for him.

Reminding herself she was better off without Wade, she spied the exit for the Wildflower Motel. The gas station was located about a mile to the north, so she turned right after getting off the interstate.

She pulled into the parking lot of the gas station, wondering how Gabe had gotten there. There was no sign of his car, a tomato-red SUV. She hadn't seen it in the motel parking lot either.

Had he taken a rideshare out there? Was that the person who'd robbed him?

She killed the engine and slid out from behind the wheel. Ducking her chin into her coat collar, she hurried inside the building. It reeked of tobacco, either from the stock of cigarettes or because the clerk smoked while on duty.

"Cassidy!" Gabe's expression brightened when he saw her. "Thanks for coming."

"What on earth happened?" Gabe's brown hair and the side of his face was matted and smeared with blood. Her heart squeezed as she realized he'd been assaulted. "Who did this to you?"

"I don't know." A flicker of uncertainty darkened his brown eyes. It took her a minute to realize he wasn't wearing his glasses. He'd recently gotten contacts but mentioned how he hadn't liked wearing them at work. "Can we please get out of here?"

"Yes, of course." She glanced at the clerk who was

watching them suspiciously. She smiled and nodded at him. "Thank you for allowing my friend to borrow your phone."

The clerk shrugged. "It is fine. Just please go now."

"Yes, thanks," Gabe added.

She took his arm and steered him toward the door. But rather than going outside, Gabe stopped, peering through the glass into the night. She frowned, wondering what was wrong with him, but then he moved forward to open the door.

"We need to hurry," he said as they stepped outside. "I don't like being out in the open like this."

What? She glanced at Gabe, wondering what on earth he was talking about. This wasn't the Gabe she knew. He was acting as if he was a cop who needed to track down a perp.

Not the tech team expert who supported her and her fellow officers while they were on scene facing adversity in their quest to protect the public.

"You're worrying me," she said as they crossed to her black SUV. "Where's your car? Was that stolen too?"

"My car?" Gabe turned in his seat, looking confused. "I don't know. What kind of car do I drive?"

Again, she felt as if she'd been dropped into an alternate universe. "You're asking me what kind of car you drive?" She frowned, searching his gaze. "You know what car you drive. You were so happy to have the only bright-red SUV in the parking lot of our precinct."

"Precinct?" Gabe clipped his seatbelt in place. "We're cops?"

"I'm a cop. You're our tech analyst." As she put the SUV into gear and pulled out of the parking lot, she didn't try to hide her frustration. "What is going on with you, Gabe? Why are you acting like this?"

He didn't answer for a long moment. "I guess I should tell you everything."

"Yes, you should." Cass braced herself. "What have you gotten involved in?"

"I don't know." Gabe lifted a hand to his head, winced, then lowered it again. "I don't know anything. I didn't remember my name until you mentioned it on the phone. I don't know why I was hit on the head and knocked unconscious. I don't know why I woke up way out in the middle of nowhere without my wallet, phone, or any cash. I don't remember anything."

Seriously? She glanced at him, trying to understand.

"I wish I could tell you what is going on, but I can't. I don't remember anyone being with me or striking out at me." He turned to meet her gaze, and the troubled expression on his face tugged at her heartstrings. "I only remember you, Cassidy."

She blew out a breath, reeling from what he was saying. Part of her wanted to scoff at the idea that he had amnesia. That Gabe Melrose couldn't remember his name or his impressive career within the tactical team.

But the man she knew wasn't this good of an actor. Gabe might be big into gaming and unreasonably excited over technological advances, but he didn't pretend to be something he wasn't. He was up front and honest about his strengths and weaknesses.

A trait she'd found endearing.

She forced herself to think like a cop. Gabe had been assaulted and robbed. And as such, he was the victim of a crime. "Okay, you have a head injury and can't remember anything. I'll take you straight to Trinity Medical Center to be medically evaluated."

"No! We can't go to the hospital." He grabbed her arm.

"Please, Cassidy, just take me home. I'm sure I'll remember everything by morning."

"Gabe, you're bleeding and have a head injury. Of course, you need to be checked out. The gash on your head likely needs stitches."

"No, please. I don't want to go." His voice sounded panicked. "Not yet."

She glanced at him with concern. "What is really going on here, Gabe?"

"I don't know." He closed his eyes for a moment, then turned to look at her. "I wish I understood why I'm in this situation. All I can say is that my gut is telling me to lie low. To keep off the grid. To make it difficult to find me."

"Who? To make it difficult for who to find you?" She didn't want to risk his head injury getting worse. But the way he was so emphatic about not going in to be seen was weighing on her. What if he was right? What if someone was still out there, waiting for the chance to finish him off?

"I don't know!" His voice was tortured. "If I knew, I'd tell you so you could help me find and arrest him!"

"Him? You remember the assailant was a man?" she asked.

He sighed heavily. "No, I don't remember. I guess it could be a woman who clocked me in the back of the head, but I assumed the person responsible was a man. Someone with the strength to toss me out of the car and onto the side of the road."

Cassidy didn't point out that she, Raelyn, and Jina, the only female members of Rhy Finnegan's tactical team, were capable of that and more. Because he was probably right. It wasn't likely the assailant was a woman, yet one thing she'd learned over the course of her career was to not make any assumptions.

She and several of her teammates had trusted the wrong person before. Anything was possible.

But that didn't help in making the right decision about whether to take him to the hospital or to give in to his request to be taken home.

"We could try to reach out to Alanna," she finally said. "I'm sure she has the ability to stitch up a wound."

"No. I can't allow you to drag anyone else into this." Gabe curled his fingers into fists, another gesture she'd never noticed from him before. He seemed very different from the Gabe she'd worked with for four years now.

"I would rather—" she began, but he cut her off.

"No. I'm begging you to take me home. If my memory is still foggy by the morning, I'll agree to be checked out." He met her gaze. "I promise."

"Fine." She threw up her hand. "Have it your way. I don't ever remember you being this stubborn before, Gabe. It's not the least bit logical not to have a doctor examine a head injury."

"I'm sorry." His tone was subdued, as if she'd wounded him by speaking her thoughts. "I can't explain it other than to say I have this weird sense that I'm in danger. That I need to remember what happened before I do anything else."

She gave in, mostly because she knew how important it was to trust her instincts. If Gabe felt as if he was in danger, then she needed to take his feelings into consideration.

"Maybe we shouldn't go to your place," she said, breaking the silence. "You can stay with me."

He hesitated. "I don't want to put you out. The thought of going home doesn't scare me the way going to the hospital does."

That didn't make any sense. Yet rather than continuing

to argue, she passed the exit that would take them to her condo and kept going toward White Gull Bay.

She'd give in to a certain extent. If he wanted to go home, she'd stay with him at his place. She knew Gabe had inherited the house from his father, who had passed away two years ago. Not only did he have a nice guest bedroom, but he was in no condition to toss her out.

For one thing, Gabe was tall and skinny, despite the way he devoured snacks like he feared a worldwide shortage loomed on the horizon. But even more so because she and Raelyn had begun working out with Jina at her MMA gym. She didn't have Jina's skill or strength yet, but she was learning.

She could be stubborn too.

"What's my last name?" Gabe's question came from left field. "If you don't mind me asking."

"Melrose. Your name is Gabriel Thomas Melrose. Your dad's name was Thomas." She glanced at him. "He died two years ago."

He frowned. "I wish I could remember him."

She had no idea what to say to that. Gabe and his father had been very close, but that wasn't the case with his mother who had remarried eighteen years ago. She'd traded up, as Gabe had put it. Giving up his father the police detective for a wealthy lawyer.

Gabe's home was a small ranch, two houses in from the corner. She pulled into the driveway, frowning when she didn't see any Christmas decorations. Gabe had mentioned his plan to put up a tree this year, but it appeared he hadn't followed through.

She parked in the driveway and slid out from behind the wheel. Gabe headed to the garage and entered a code on the keypad. Which was probably a good thing since he'd been robbed and didn't have his keys.

When the garage door opened, though, she saw his red SUV parked inside. What in the world? Gabe had clearly left the car behind on purpose.

He looked just as surprised to see the SUV. He glanced at her. "This is my car?"

"Yes." Alarm bells rang in the back of her mind, and she reached for her gun. "Stay back. I'm going in first."

He scowled, looking as if he wanted to argue, but stepped to the side to give her room to squeeze past the car. The door leading from the garage to the house didn't look tampered with, but she didn't lower her weapon. Twisting the handle, she pushed the door open but hung back to wait and listen.

Hearing nothing, she stepped across the threshold, sweeping her gun over the area as she went. It was dark inside, but lights from the neighbors' Christmas decorations along with the streetlight outside, provided enough illumination for her to see.

The interior of the house stopped her cold. The place had been trashed. Her gaze went from the shattered over-sized TV screen to the sofa cushions that had been cut open and strewn around the room to the kitchen drawers that had been opened and dumped onto the floor.

This was no robbery. Whoever had done this had been searching for something. She only wished she knew exactly what they'd wanted.

CHAPTER TWO

He shouldn't have come here.

Over Cassidy's shoulder, Gabe could see the destroyed interior of his home. Then he realized something was missing.

"My computer." He brushed past Cass to stride into the kitchen. Or what was left of his kitchen. "My laptop computer is gone."

"Good to know but stay back," she warned, grabbing his arm in a firm grip. "I need to make sure the assailant isn't hiding somewhere."

That possibility hadn't occurred to him. "Okay, I'll wait."

"Don't touch anything." Cassidy moved through the open-concept kitchen and living room to head down the hall toward the bedrooms. He felt useless standing there, but since he didn't have a gun, there wasn't anything he could do to help.

Did he own a gun? He frowned. Somehow, he couldn't imagine using a weapon, pointing and aiming at a person.

Yet even as that image wouldn't mesh in his mind, he found himself wishing he was armed.

If someone tried to harm Cassidy, he wouldn't hesitate to use any weapon at hand.

"Bedrooms are clear," she announced. "If you had a computer on your desk in the office, that is missing as well."

The news was like a fist punch to the gut. He wasn't sure why, but knowing his computers had been taken brought a wave of depression. As if he'd lost his right hand.

"Hang tight," Cassidy said. "I'll check the basement."

He turned to look at the door leading to the basement. Interesting that he knew exactly where it was. And that his laptop was missing. His desktop device, too, apparently. Slowly but surely, memories were coming back in bits and pieces.

Maybe all he needed was a good night's sleep. Surely by morning he'd remember everything that had transpired out at the side of the road. And the source of the danger he was convinced lurked nearby.

Maybe.

He moved to the kitchen sink, grabbed a towel, and ran it under cold water. The ache in his head would not go away, so he used the wet towel to wipe away the blood.

"You weren't supposed to touch anything," Cass chided when she returned.

"I highly doubt the crime scene techs will find any prints." He glanced around while holding the cold towel to the back of his head, trying to make sense of this. But more memories didn't come. "I should grab a few clothes and some money so we can get out of here. I wouldn't bother changing except mine have blood stains on them."

Cassidy sighed, then nodded in agreement. "Okay, but

don't take too long. We'll call dispatch to report the damage once we're back on the road."

He tossed the blood-stained towel aside and headed toward the bedrooms, turning into the one he used without conscious thought. It was only when he had grabbed a small suitcase from the closet and began stuffing clothing in that he realized he knew exactly where he stored things.

Progress in his memory returning? He could only hope.

He also found a small wad of cash in his top dresser drawer. Not a very original hiding place, but when he looked inside, the money was still there. It was only about a thousand dollars, but better than nothing.

Less than five minutes later, he joined Cass in the kitchen, rolling the small carry-on suitcase behind him. She turned and led the way back outside. He took a moment to use the keypad to close the garage door, then asked, "How do you think they got inside?"

"No sign of forced entry," Cassidy said with a shrug. "Could be they somehow got your key code information."

He didn't think his key code was common knowledge; his house didn't appear to have had any repairs lately indicating he may have given it out to a worker. Yet thanks to his inability to remember anything, he couldn't say for sure he hadn't shared it with someone.

Maybe even the same person who'd driven him outside of town, clubbed him on the head, and left him to die.

He abruptly stopped midstride. Had he known his assailant? Was that the reason he'd gotten into the car with him?

Not being able to remember was infuriating. He needed his brain to heal and fast.

Before it was too late.

Too late for what, he wasn't sure.

"Gabe? Is something wrong?" Cassidy's voice penetrated his troubled thoughts.

"No. I'm fine." He opened the rear hatch, set his suitcase inside, and closed it again. He slid into the passenger seat as Cassidy started the engine. As they drove away, he turned to glance back at the house. He wouldn't have been able to give Cass directions on how to get there, but he was relieved to discover the inside was familiar.

It occurred to him that he might be able to jog his memory by looking at photographs of people he knew. To do that, he'd need a computer. Maybe Cassidy had one he could borrow. The previous sense of urgency he experienced upon waking up at the side of the road returned with a vengeance.

As if there was something important he had to do. Maybe even something related to his computer.

When Cassidy took the on-ramp to the interstate, he asked, "Where are we going?"

"My place." Then she hit the phone button on her steering wheel. "Call dispatch."

He heard the other end of a phone ringing, then a voice answered, "This is precinct seven."

"This is Officer Cassidy Sommer. I'm calling to report a break-in at the following address." She rattled it off from memory, a feat he couldn't do despite how the house belonged to him. "I understand the location is in White Gull Bay, but the home belongs to our tech analyst, Gabe Melrose. His computers are missing, and those devices are used in conjunction with our network."

"Understood. I'll send uniforms to the scene," the dispatcher said.

"Thank you. I'll make sure Captain Finnegan is aware

as well." Cassidy glanced at him as she ended the call. "Do you remember our boss?"

He grimaced. "Not really."

"How is it that you remembered me?" Cassidy asked. "Not just me personally, but also my phone number?"

He flushed with embarrassment and hoped she wouldn't notice in the darkness. "I don't know why you popped into my head. Maybe I was thinking of calling you before I lost consciousness."

"That makes sense," she said. "It's a good thing you were able to get to the gas station to make the call."

"Yeah." There was no denying the malicious intent. Whoever had dumped him at the side of the road had likely expected he'd succumb to hypothermia before he could be rescued. "I guess God was watching over me."

She snapped her head over to look at him. "I've never heard you say that. I didn't realize you believed in God."

"I, uh . . ." He wasn't sure how to respond to that. Did he believe in God? He must, otherwise why would he have said that? The phrase had come to him before he could consider what it meant. But even as he repeated the words in his mind, they felt right. He put a hand to his throbbing head. "I think so, yes. But I really wish I could remember."

Her expression softened, and she reached over to pat his knee. "You will. Give it time."

Time. He swallowed hard, instinctively knowing he didn't have time to sit around, waiting for his memory to return.

He needed to understand what was going on before the assailant struck again.

CASSIDY NEEDED to call Rhy but hated the idea of waking him up at the late hour of eleven thirty at night. His wife, Devon, was pregnant and due in the middle of January, and they had a one-year-old daughter, Colleen.

Was the loss of Gabe's laptop a security risk? Could the person who broke into his house and trashed the place access the police database? They each had their own computer passwords, but she wasn't enough of a computer geek to understand if that was enough.

Gabe was the expert in that area, but she hated to put more pressure on him. She felt bad enough about not insisting he go to the hospital.

After seeing what had been done to his house, she had decided against forcing the issue. She didn't know who had assaulted Gabe or why, but she sensed he was right about staying under the radar.

But if his memory didn't return by morning, she'd insist he get checked out. She felt certain Rhy would back her on that too. Maybe she could wait until morning to call him. Things may have changed for the better by then.

"Where are we headed?" Gabe asked.

"My place. I have a condo in Greenland. It should be safe enough for tonight."

He glanced at her. "Have I been there before?"

She arched a brow, then nodded slowly. It must be difficult to not remember basic things you'd done. Places you'd been. People you worked with. It was concerning to her that Gabe didn't remember Rhy, their tactical team captain, whom he worked very closely with on a daily basis, but had remembered her. Not just her name, but her phone number. "Yes, you drove me home a few times when my car needed repairs."

"Oh. Okay." He glanced around with interest. "Maybe I'll recognize it when I see it."

She hoped he would, but when she headed down her street to the cluster of condos lining the west side of the road, he didn't say anything. When she pulled into the driveway, he sighed.

"Guess not," he muttered half to himself.

Once they were inside, he paused. "You said I dropped you off. Have I been inside?"

"Just once. Why, does it look familiar?"

"Not really." He turned to look at her. "Do you want me to sleep on the sofa?"

"No, I have a guest room." Jina had lived with her for several weeks prior to moving in with her then fiancé now husband, Cole Robertson, after a fire had destroyed her home. Something the old Gabe would have known. "Follow me, I'll show you the way. The guest room has its own bathroom."

"You have a very nice place," Gabe said as she flicked on the light. "I appreciate you allowing me to stay."

She squelched a flash of annoyance. It wasn't Gabe's fault that he didn't remember their friendship the way she did. "Anytime. Any of the other members of the team would do the same thing."

That seemed to surprise him. He lifted his suitcase onto the bed. "I was thinking we should look through pictures, see if they spark my memories."

"Now? It's a little late." She regarded him thoughtfully. "Is this your way of asking to borrow my computer?"

"Yes. I was hoping you had one," he admitted.

She hesitated. "I'm not sure you should be looking at a computer screen while suffering from a head injury. I think you should get some sleep first. We can go through pictures tomorrow, hopefully when you're feeling better."

He looked as if he wanted to argue but then sighed. "Okay. You might be right. My head is killing me."

"Get some rest." She gave him a quick hug. "I'm glad you're okay. And I'm sure you'll feel better by morning."

"Good night, Cassidy." His voice was low and husky in a way she'd never heard from him before. Then again, the poor guy could barely remember his own name.

She closed the guest room door behind her, then crossed the hall to her room. Pulling out her phone, she was about to plug it into the charger when a text from Rhy popped up on the screen.

What's going on?

She should have known the dispatcher would call if she didn't. She texted back. *Gabe was assaulted and his home broken into. Laptop and other personal items were stolen.*

An instant later, her phone buzzed with an incoming call. "Cass? How is Gabe? Who assaulted him?" Rhy demanded.

"Sorry, I would have called, but I didn't want to wake you and Devon," she said. "I am concerned, though." She quickly filled Rhy in on the sequence of events. "We're at my place now, and I'm hoping his memory returns by morning."

"Amnesia isn't common." Rhy spoke in a hushed tone. "Back when my brother Quinn's wife, Sami, had amnesia, it took several days for her memory to return."

Days? She winced. "Well, let's hope it doesn't take that long for Gabe." She couldn't think of a way to explain how different Gabe seemed now, so she didn't mention it. "I'm encouraged by the fact that he remembered me and my number. I hate to think about what would have happened if he hadn't been able to get in touch with one of us."

"Yeah, that is troubling. Why was he all the way out near the Wildflower Motel in the first place?" Rhy asked.

"No idea. And his car is in the garage at his place, so he must have gotten a ride or taken a rideshare. His phone is missing, along with his wallet, but I was thinking it might be good to get his phone records to trace his actions prior to the assault."

"Yeah, only Gabe is the one I'd usually ask to take care of that." Rhy sighed. "We'll work on that first thing in the morning."

"Sounds like a plan." It felt good to know there were actions they could take to get to the bottom of this. "And once Gabe's memory returns, that will help us figure out what happened too."

"I'll pray for him," Rhy said. "In the meantime, get some sleep. Oh, and you should probably check on Gabe throughout the night. I think that was what Quinn did for Sami when she was injured."

"Good to know. I really wanted to take him to Trinity Medical Center, but he refused."

"They would have done a CT scan of his head to make sure there was no internal bleeding," Rhy said. "But as far as the amnesia side of things, there wasn't much the doc did for Sami. If his condition doesn't improve, we'll make sure he goes in to be seen tomorrow."

"I'll need you to give him the order," she said. "He emphatically told me his instincts were telling him to stay off the grid."

"He said that?" Rhy sounded surprised. "That's strange."

"Tell me about it." There were several aspects to the

Gabe she'd picked up tonight that didn't mesh with the man she knew. "He was right, though, based on the extent of damage found at his place. I was worried his laptop might be used to access the precinct."

"It should be well protected," Rhy said. "And again, Gabe is the one who would know that better than I would."

There was a brief pause as that sank in. Was this part of the reason Gabe was targeted? Because someone wanted to eliminate him to get access to the inner workings of the Seventh Precinct?

It didn't make sense, but they needed to keep all options open.

"Just because his memory is broken doesn't mean he won't know the computer side of things," she finally said. "We'll talk to him about this in more detail tomorrow."

"Okay. Good night, Cass."

"Good night." She ended the call, plugged her phone into the charger, then set an alarm for three hours from now.

She closed her eyes and prayed Gabe's condition would improve and that his memory would return.

When her alarm went off, she bolted upright, her heart thumping. Normally, she didn't need an alarm, her internal clock was set for six a.m., and she always woke up on her own.

But it was three in the morning, not six. She tiptoed from her room and carefully opened Gabe's door. He appeared to be asleep, his head on the pillow. He'd covered the pillow with a towel to protect the pillowcase from being stained with blood.

As if she cared about that when he was injured. Shaking her head, she moved silently across the room until she was near the bed. She hated to disturb him, but if Rhy thought he needed to be awoken frequently, then that's what she'd do.

"Gabe?" she whispered as she placed a hand on his shoulder.

He reacted as if she'd stuck him with a hot poker, rearing up and spinning toward her with his hand lifted as if to strike out. Caught off guard, she reared back to avoid being hit.

"Who's there?" Gabe asked.

"It's me. Cassidy." She put her hand out. "Take it easy, you're safe."

"Cassidy." He let out a heavy sigh, then scrubbed his hands over his face. "Sorry about that. I—was confused for a moment."

"It's my fault." She took a step closer so he could see her better. "I spoke to Rhy, and he mentioned that when his sister-in-law Sami had amnesia, the doctor advised waking her throughout the night."

"I see. I didn't realize Rhy had experience with this sort of thing." He grimaced. "I don't really remember him, but I get the sense I should."

"Yes, you work very closely with Rhy." She rested her hand on his shoulder. "How's the headache?"

"A little better." He managed a lopsided smile. "I'm sorry I almost hit you."

"You didn't." Although she was still reeling over how fast Gabe had reacted. It was something she'd never seen him do before. He was normally an easygoing guy. His comfort zone was his office, functioning as their computer expert, a virtual whiz at decoding technology. He was always ready and able to assist their tactical team in every way, often working late into the evening when things were not going well.

It was disconcerting to see him as a victim. Especially one determined to protect himself.

"Go back to sleep," she said. "I won't wake you until six."

"Okay." He hesitated, then added, "Good night, Cass."

It was the same low, husky voice he'd used earlier, and hearing it sent shivers down her spine.

"Good night." She quickly turned away. What was wrong with her? Since when was she attracted to Gabe Melrose?

He was her friend. Not a potential date. End of story.

Maybe she needed a CT scan of her head too.

After resetting her alarm, she crawled back into bed. This time, sleep didn't come easily, and she stared up at her ceiling for a full hour before drifting off. When her alarm blared, she groaned out loud.

Shaking off her fatigue, she decided to take a shower, change her clothes, and dry her hair before waking up Gabe. One thing she knew for certain was how much he liked to eat. His desk drawer was always stuffed with snacks.

"Gabe?" She made sure to stand a few feet away from the bed this time. "Gabe, it's Cassidy. Time to wake up."

Thankfully, he didn't react as if she were his assailant this time. He groaned and rolled over, blinking at her. "Hey. You're clear, not fuzzy."

Her eyes widened with concern. "I don't understand what you're talking about. Are you okay? Is your headache worse?"

"No, I'm fine. I meant I can see you clearly." He lifted his hands to his eyes. "I'm not wearing my glasses. I usually do, right?"

"Yes." That made her relax. "I noticed that last night.

You recently got contact lenses. Although I'm not sure why you decided to go down that path."

His brow puckered, but he shrugged. "Maybe I wanted to see clearly when I woke up."

"Makes sense to me." Reassured his memory was returning, she turned away to give him some privacy. "I'll start breakfast while you wash up."

It was still dark outside at this hour, so she flicked on the kitchen light. She normally ate oatmeal with fruit but decided to make eggs and toast, adding the fruit as a side.

Despite her lack of sleep, she hummed under her breath as she worked, anticipating a productive day ahead of them. Once they knew who had attacked Gabe, she and her teammates would work quickly to find and arrest the person responsible.

Her coffee maker was set ahead of time to brew at exactly six o'clock, so the pot was already made. She sipped the steaming brew as she worked. She placed cut strawberries and blueberries in a large bowl, then set about making scrambled eggs. While they cooked, she dropped four slices of bread into the toaster.

When Gabe entered the kitchen, she was struck by how handsome he was. It was odd to notice his looks now when she saw him every day. "Something smells great."

"Have a seat." She poured him a cup of coffee. "Breakfast is just about ready."

"Do you eat like this every morning?" Gabe asked, eyeing the fruit and the two plates of eggs and toast she set before him.

"No, but you deserve it." She sat beside him. "I'm so glad you're feeling better."

"Me too." He eyed her over the rim of his cup. "My

headache isn't as bad as it was. I just wish my memory would come back."

She tried to mask her disappointment. "I thought your memory had returned."

"Nope." He set his coffee aside, then folded his hands in his lap and bowed his head. It took her a moment to realize he was waiting for her to say grace.

"Dear Lord Jesus, we thank You for providing this food we are about to eat. We also thank You for keeping Gabe safe in Your care. We ask You to please heal his memory too. Amen."

"Amen," he echoed. Then he grinned. "Dig in."

That was a phrase Roscoe had coined back when he'd joined the team, making them laugh when he said it after every prayer. Hearing Gabe repeat it gave her hope that his memory would return in full. Maybe the key was to keep him preoccupied with other things. It seemed his memory worked better when he wasn't pushing himself to recall details about the assault.

They ate in silence for several minutes. She tried not to stare at him, even though she was acutely aware of seeing him in a different light.

"This is great, Cass," he said.

"You're welcome." She cradled her coffee mug in her hands. "Rhy will want me to take you to Trinity Medical Center, so we'll do that first. From there, I'll take you to the precinct."

He frowned. "I don't need to go to the hospital. But heading to the precinct is a good idea. Maybe being there will spur my memory."

That was a good point, but she had her orders. "Rhy's the boss."

Gabe looked annoyed. "I'll talk to Rhy." Before she could say anything more, he jumped to his feet, only to sway for a moment. "Too fast. Dizzy," he murmured as he sank back down at the same moment a bullet shattered the window.

"Down, get down!" She yanked Gabe off the chair and shoved him under the table, realizing with sick certainty that she'd been wrong to bring Gabe to her place.

The assailant must have known enough about the team to have found them. And clearly this perp's intent was to finish what he'd started.

Eliminating Gabe as a threat, permanently.

CHAPTER THREE

Gabe's heart thundered in his chest. He wasn't sure if he'd ever been in a dangerous situation like this before but decided he didn't much like it. Realizing Cassidy had her weapon in hand, he quickly grabbed her arm. "Don't. Stay here."

"Take my phone and call 911." She thumbed the screen, then thrust the device into his free hand. She shook off his grasp. "Keep your head down. I need to find the shooter."

He'd known that was her intent. "Please don't. What if there's more than one out there?" As he spoke, he pressed 911 on the phone screen. "They might be coordinating their efforts to draw you out."

She frowned. "Do you remember there being more than one assailant?"

He didn't remember anything, and that was the most frustrating thing of all. He couldn't shake the feeling that it was urgent he remember what he was doing when this all started. Yet his mind was nothing but fog.

"This is 911, please state your emergency."

"Shots fired in Greenland. Send backup!" His voice rose in alarm.

When asked for the address, he rattled it off, easily remembering it from when they'd arrived yesterday. Ironic that he could remember everything since he'd woken up at the side of the road, but nothing from prior to that.

Nothing that really mattered.

"Officers have been dispatched to the area," the dispatcher said in her eerily serene voice. He assumed she did that to keep the victims calm, and the strategy worked. His pulse settled down now that he knew help was on the way. "Please stay on the line."

"Okay." He set the phone on the floor, relieved that Cassidy hadn't left to investigate. However, she had her head up above the kitchen table, looking around. He couldn't see what had caught her attention. "What's wrong?"

"Shots came through the front window," she said in a low voice. "We may be able to leave through the back."

He shouldn't have been surprised she was planning an escape route. Cass appeared as calm as the dispatcher.

As if she was pinned down by gunfire on a regular basis. Which now that he thought about it, she probably was.

"We should wait for backup to arrive." He didn't want her to become a target too. Whatever was going on involved him. He was the one who'd dragged her into the line of fire. Because she was the only person he'd remembered.

Guilt washed over him. If Rhy was his boss, why hadn't he remembered him?

"I don't like sitting here," Cassidy said, clearly frustrated. "We can't let this shooter get away."

He could appreciate her concern. "Do you have a second weapon for me? I'd feel better if I could back you up."

She dropped down to stare at him in shock. "You want a weapon?"

Was that an unusual request? He had no clue. "Yes. I feel like I should be armed in case . . ." He swallowed hard.

In case something happened to Cassidy.

"Do you know how to shoot?" She still looked dumbfounded by his request.

"I don't know. I don't remember." He was tired of saying those words. "Maybe I can't hit what I'm aiming at, but I might be able to use the gun as a deterrent. I hate feeling naked and afraid."

She sent him an exasperated glance. "I can't give a gun to someone who doesn't know how to use it."

Maybe she was right to take that approach. What did he know? The wail of sirens indicated the police were on the way. Relief in knowing they would soon be safe washed over him.

Relatively speaking. He knew the danger would never be over until the black hole of his memory was filled in with colorful images of what had happened to him.

"Stay here for a while longer." Cassidy abruptly stood and moved away. It was all Gabe could do not to follow.

"Anyone hurt?" a cop shouted.

"We're fine. Any sign of the shooter?" Cassidy called back.

"Negative. We'll search the perimeter," the cop responded.

Gabe clenched his jaw, hating that the shooter or shooters had gotten away. Not to mention how they'd shot right through Cassidy's window. It occurred to him that he should disappear on his own, find a place to stay, and hunker down until his memory returned.

But what if it didn't? He had refused to get checked out at the hospital, so he didn't really know what the doctor would say about the possibility of his memory returning.

"Clear!"

"Clear!"

"Clear!" The third voice was Cassidy's. Feeling like an idiot, he crawled out from beneath the kitchen table and headed for the front door.

It opened before he could reach it. Two officers looked at him in confusion for a moment, until Cassidy came in through the back door.

"Thanks for responding so quickly." She nodded to the officers. "This is the intended victim, Gabe Melrose. He's a tech analyst for MPD and was recently assaulted and left for dead. The bullet missed him by inches." She turned to gesture to the kitchen cabinet. Gabe was shocked to see a round hole where a bullet was lodged. "That's the slug. There was a second shot, too, but I'm not sure where that one landed."

Hearing the discussion surrounding the attempt on his life was surreal. He assumed in his position as tech analyst he wasn't often the victim of a crime.

Until now.

"Okay, we'll get this removed and processed as evidence," the older of the two officers said.

"I would like to be updated about the progress of your investigation," Cassidy said. "This is my condo, but there was also a break-in at Gabe's home in White Gull Bay. Both crimes are in different jurisdictions, so the results need to be shared among those of us who are involved."

The older cop grimaced but nodded. "Yeah, sure. We know how things work when Rhy Finnegan calls the shots."

Maybe the comment wasn't meant to be derogatory, but Gabe found himself stepping forward, leveling the cop with a grim stare. "Watch it. Rhy Finnegan is a great cop who has solved dozens of cases."

"Yeah, he's a glory hound all right," the younger cop muttered. "Stealing the big cases right out from under us."

"It's not like that." Cassidy put her hand on his arm, subtly tugging him back. "Rhy can't help it when cases that involve members of our tactical team cross jurisdictions. If I lived in Milwaukee, this wouldn't even be an issue."

"But you don't," the older cop said. "You choose to live here in Greenland. In our jurisdiction."

Gabe couldn't explain why this sounded like a conversation that he'd heard before. There was a sense of familiarity about the argument over jurisdictions. Either way, he was annoyed by the inane comments. He glared at the officers. "All that matters is finding and arresting those responsible. Right?"

They all glanced at him in surprise. Finally, the older cop shrugged. "Yeah. Sure. That's what counts."

"Good." Gabe glanced at Cassidy. "Is it too early to call Rhy?"

"I think we need to get you out of here first," she said. "We'll head to the precinct; it's about the only place where I can keep you safe."

"Hold on, we'd like to know more about the break-in at the victim's home," the older cop protested. "What happened? Was anything taken?"

Gabe hesitated, then caught the tiny nod Cassidy gave, indicating he should fill them in on the details. "Yes, both my laptop and desktop computers were stolen. My big screen TV was also busted into dozens of pieces, along with my gaming system. A state-of-the-art gaming system," he added somewhat bitterly. "And the place was ransacked."

"The TV and gaming system were busted up?" The younger cop frowned. "Doesn't sound like the motive is money. The burglars could have made a decent amount selling them for cash."

"I agree; this isn't about easy cash," Cassidy said. "Since Gabe works as our computer expert, I'm worried his computers were taken to gain access to our police database. Maybe even to see what Gabe was recently working on."

The older cop whistled. "That would not be good."

"No, it isn't," Cass agreed. "You can see why it's important we all work together on this moving forward. Cooperating with a joint investigation is imperative if we're going to find and arrest these guys."

"More than one?" the younger cop asked.

"I don't know." Gabe hated not having answers. It gave him the impression that he was usually in a position of having knowledge at his fingertips.

The more he thought about his stolen computers, the more concerned he grew about the assailant's intent. Access to the police database was one thing, but taking shots at him escalated the danger to a whole new level.

He lightly touched the goose egg on the back of his head. Somehow, the key to this was hidden deep in his mind.

If only he could find a way to retrieve it.

CASSIDY NOTICED GABE fingering the back of his head. "Do you need ice?"

"No. It's fine." He dropped his hand as if he'd been caught stealing. "I like your idea of heading to the precinct. Maybe seeing my stuff would help me remember."

"Remember what?" Officer Yanny was younger than Officer Brown and, in Cassidy's opinion, the more unreasonable of the two. His comment about Rhy being a glory hound couldn't be further from the truth.

Rhy was the best boss she'd ever worked for. The kind of guy who cared about those under his command. He made sure they toed the line, but he was also the first one rushing into danger alongside them as needed.

"I don't remember who attacked me." Gabe waved his hand. "It's not important. I'm sure my memory will return soon."

Cassidy wished she believed that. But it seemed to her that the longer Gabe couldn't remember, the less likely it was that he would recall the attack at all.

She didn't know of anything specific that Gabe had been working on for the team, and Rhy hadn't mentioned that possibility either. Was it possible someone else in the precinct had asked Gabe to dig into something suspicious? If so, she hoped they'd get a clue when they reached the precinct. Gabe would be able to log into his computer there to hopefully find what they needed.

"We need your contact information," Officer Brown said. "In case we have more questions."

"I don't have my phone or my wallet," Gabe said.

"I'll give you my number. You can reach Gabe through me." She patted her pockets, realizing she didn't have her phone. Then she remembered giving it to Gabe when he was ducking for cover. Spying it lying on the floor under the table, she bent to retrieve it. "Or you can reach us at the Seventh Precinct in Milwaukee." She waited until Brown had pulled out his phone to provide her phone number. He dutifully plugged it into his list of contacts.

"Do you have anything we can use to board up the window?" Gabe asked. "I don't want to leave it like this."

She was about to say no, then remembered there were a few sheets of plywood down in the basement. She had a secret jigsaw puzzle habit and used the plywood as a table across her hassock so she could do the puzzle while watching TV. It was something she'd done to help combat the memories from last month when she'd been forced to kill a perp.

"Yes, I'll grab it." She resisted the urge to glance at her watch. Taking a few extra minutes to secure her condo was worth it.

"I'll help you." Gabe followed her down the stairs. The condo was only four years old, so the area was fairly clean.

And empty, except for the normal basement stuff like her washer, dryer, hot water heater, furnace, and, of course, the two sheets of plywood.

Gabe grabbed one end, leaving her to take the other. Together they carried the planks up the stairs and to the main living space. "I have a small tool kit," she said, turning away.

To her surprise, Gabe took the hammer and nails to do the repair. She hadn't pictured him as being the handy sort, but then again, she was most familiar with his computer skills. The plywood covering the windows wouldn't keep anyone super determined from getting inside, but that was the least of her worries.

How had the gunman found them there? She made sure they weren't followed, and the shooter hadn't shown up until several hours later. Although she had to admit, they'd struck just before dawn, so maybe they had been outside the entire time, waiting for the perfect shot.

If Gabe hadn't gotten dizzy, he might have been killed right in front of her eyes. The image was so horrifying she had to take a deep breath and look away.

She cared about Gabe; he was a valued colleague and genuinely nice guy. They were friends, so this odd awareness of him had to be a result of the situation. Nothing more. She'd be upset if any of their teammates had been targeted.

Ironically, most of them had been under fire at one point or another. Most recently, Flynn and his fiancée, Taylor, had been the ones in danger.

Never in her wildest dreams had she considered Gabe Melrose would become a target.

When her phone rang, she pulled it from her pocket. Seeing Rhy's name on the screen made her wonder if their boss had X-ray vision and already knew about the shooting. She caught Gabe's gaze as she answered. "Hey, Rhy."

"I heard about a shooting in Greenland," Rhy said, getting straight to the point. "Are you and Gabe okay?"

"We're fine. But my condo took a couple of bullets." She gestured for Gabe to come closer. He'd finished putting up the plywood with an ease that impressed her. "We were just about to head down to the precinct to fill you in."

"I'm heading there now and can pick you up on the way," Rhy said. "I'd rather you don't use your vehicle. Or Gabe's for that matter."

It was a good point. Gabe's car was still in his garage, and she understood the need to leave hers behind too. "I guess it's our turn to use the undercover Jeep," she said. "We'll wait here for you to swing by. Thanks for the offer."

"Be there in ten." Rhy ended the call without saying anything more.

"Your boss is coming here?" Officer Yanny looked annoyed. "Guess it didn't take long for him to get his fingers on the case."

Gabe stepped forward again, clearly upset. "He's coming here to drive us to the precinct. Something I'm sure your boss has never done."

Yanny looked as if he might argue, but then he turned away. She took Gabe's arm and drew him aside. "It's okay. Rhy doesn't need us to protect him."

"Yeah, well, they're making me mad." Gabe shot the two officers a perturbed look. "I don't understand why they're being so stupid. What does it matter who does what as long as we find the guy responsible?"

"It's just that most cops are territorial." She had to smile, realizing this was probably the first time Gabe had been on this end of a crime scene. "Think about how upset we would be if someone tried to take over a case that we had done most of the work on."

"They haven't done much work from what I can tell," Gabe muttered.

"It will fine." She blew out a breath. "Grab your suitcase. I'll throw some stuff in my gym bag too. We won't be coming back here anytime soon."

He grimaced. "I guess not."

She followed him down the hall to their respective rooms. After packing her gym bag with clean clothes, she removed the lock box from beneath her bed. She had a backup weapon, most cops did, but she wasn't sure giving it to Gabe was a smart idea.

He'd never used a weapon before in his life as far as she

knew. Then again, he'd surprised her by how easily he secured the plywood over her shattered window.

Had she and the rest of the team underestimated Gabe? He was highly valued for his skills feeding them key information when they needed it the most. But she had always imagined he spent his days snacking while glued to his computer at home. Especially since he was always talking about the latest video games.

In truth, she hadn't liked Gabe's penchant for video games. Her stepbrothers were big into gaming, and it seemed a rather juvenile way to spend their time.

Whatever. With a shrug, she tucked her spare weapon and an extra clip in the duffel bag. She was hopeful that once they'd arrived at the precinct, the familiar surroundings would spark a return of Gabe's missing memories.

Slinging the duffel over her shoulder, she returned to the living room. Gabe's suitcase was set against the wall as he washed dishes in the sink.

Gabe. Washing her dishes. Now she really felt as if she'd been dropped into an alternative universe.

"You don't have to do that," she protested. "Just let them soak in the water. I can take care of them later."

"We don't know how long this will take." He glanced at her with a grim expression. "I feel bad, like this is all my fault. If I could remember anything useful, we wouldn't be in this predicament."

"Not true," she said. "Other members of the team have been in danger over the past year from unknown assailants as well. This isn't your fault."

"I feel like it is," he said, continuing to wash the dishes. "And I'm not happy that I've inadvertently put you in danger too."

It was on the tip of her tongue to point out she was always in danger, but a car pulling into the driveway caught her attention. The plywood wasn't as soundproof as her windows.

Instantly, she crossed to the window that wasn't broken and peered outside. She relaxed when she saw Rhy's familiar features. He'd gotten out of the car and was speaking with the officers on scene.

"Leave the dishes, Gabe. Rhy's here." She crossed over to grab his rolling suitcase.

He nodded but finished what he was doing. He rinsed the dishes and then dried his hands on a towel. "I'm ready. They can air dry."

"Let's go, then." She slung her duffel over her shoulder, opened the front door, and stepped out to meet Rhy. Her boss's gaze went from her to Gabe, who loomed behind her. He was taller than her by at least five inches.

"Gabe. I hear you've had some trouble," Rhy said by way of greeting.

"You could say that." Gabe brought his suitcase as he stepped onto the porch beside her. "It's good to see you, Rhy."

She turned to gape at him. "Your memory returned?"

"I remember Rhy now that I see him," Gabe said. "But the events from the assault are still a black hole."

"I'm glad you remember me." Rhy managed a smile as he pulled the suitcase and duffel from her fingers. "I hope that's a sign the rest of your memories will return soon. Meanwhile, let's get out of here."

They stored their suitcase and duffel. Gabe took the back seat, leaving her to sit up front with Rhy. "Did Yanny and Brown give you any trouble?" she asked as Rhy backed out of the driveway.

"No, why would they?" he asked with a frown.

"No reason." She turned to glance back at Gabe. "Told you they were all talk and no action."

Gabe nodded but didn't say anything. He seemed to be studying Rhy's profile, as if willing more memories to the surface.

Since Rhy didn't mention taking Gabe to the hospital, she let it go. Other than his memory loss and a headache, Gabe seemed fine. His scalp wound might still need stitches, though. And he had been momentarily dizzy.

Maybe they could stop by an urgent care clinic on the way to—wherever they'd end up spending the night.

"I heard there's a bullet embedded in your cabinet," Rhy said, breaking into her thoughts. "They were waiting for the crime scene techs to retrieve it."

She nodded. "It's possible we'll be able to match it with a weapon in the system, but I'm not holding my breath. It is a mistake, though, and hopefully, if these guys keep coming after Gabe, they'll make another."

"Guys plural?" Rhy asked.

"I don't know for sure since I can't remember," Gabe said, his tone testy.

"Okay, okay. Just asking if you saw more than one shooter," Rhy said.

"I didn't see anyone," Cassidy admitted.

"Me either," Gabe added.

Rhy nodded and made short work of the trip to their precinct. He pulled around the building to park in the back lot, which was partially hidden from the street. Normally, their precinct was a safety zone, but there had been instances where bad guys had camped outside the building to shoot at them.

Never a dull moment in law enforcement, she thought as

she followed Rhy and Gabe inside. Yet that variety was also what she loved most about being on the job.

That and making the world a better place. At least their small portion of the world.

"This looks familiar," Gabe said, his tone full of excitement. "My office is over there." He gestured with a hand. "And the break room is there." He turned toward it.

"I'm glad things are starting to come back to you," Rhy said. "Don't force yourself to remember, just let the thoughts come naturally."

"Yeah, okay." Gabe's expression turned thoughtful. "I hope that happens soon, though. I can't seem to shake off the strange sense of urgency."

Rhy met her gaze, lifting a brow as if asking what he was talking about. She could only shrug. "We'll know when he does," she said.

"Do you think you can log into your computer?" Rhy asked. "Maybe that will give us a clue as to what you've been working on."

Gabe didn't answer but headed to his office. He dropped into his chair, looked around, then booted up the computer. When the log-in page bloomed on the screen, he placed his fingertips on the keyboard and began to type.

She held her breath as she watched over his shoulder. There was a spinning wheel for a moment, then the main screen popped up.

"You did it!" The words were barely out of her mouth when suddenly the screen went white, then red, then black. "What happened?"

Gabe hit several keys, trying to get the home screen to come back, but it was no use.

"Hey, what happened? I've been booted off the system," one of the cops said.

"Me too!" another responded. "I can't get my computer to work."

"I have a bad feeling my logging in has sent a virus through the system," Gabe said, his tone hoarse. "We've been sabotaged."

Sabotaged? She looked at Rhy, who had gone pale.

Was this the reason Gabe had been assaulted? To destroy his work?

Or was there something much more sinister at play?

CHAPTER FOUR

"Can you fix it?" Rhy asked.

Gabe glanced at his boss, who looked very concerned. "I'll do my best." He raked a hand through his hair, then winced when his fingers brushed against the goose egg. He felt awful for inadvertently unleashing a virus. Should he have anticipated that? He wasn't sure if he would have considered that as a possible threat even if he had his memory. Unless his memory included finding a virus in the first place. Yet if that was the case, he would have reported it.

"I'll call Assistant Chief Michaels." Rhy glanced at Cass, then back to Gabe. "I don't mean to pressure you, but we really need your expertise to get us back up and running. Thanks to the changes you made in the system last year, this should only impact our precinct. Not all of them."

The thought of all the precincts in the entire city of Milwaukee going down gave him a chill. Talk about a crippling blow against law enforcement. He gestured to the computer. "I'll get to work on this right away."

"Thanks." Rhy turned to head to his office, but Cassidy hung back.

"Are you sure you're up to this?" Her voice was low so as not to carry. "I'm not a medical professional, but I've heard screen time is not good for concussions."

"I'm fine." He forced a smile, touched by her concern. "Sounds like I should know this system backward and forward."

"You do," she said with confidence. "But you're not a robot either. Just be careful. Don't push yourself too much."

"I won't." He told himself there was no time to bask in her concern. He turned his attention back on the computer. Despite the holes in his memory, he knew exactly how to access the system's basic operating system. A few keystrokes later, he was in and able to navigate around. In familiar territory now, he searched for the virus that had infected their departmental system.

At some point, Cass brought him more coffee. "Thanks," he said absently, without taking his gaze from the screen. "I appreciate your support."

"That's our line when it comes to the work you do for us," Cassidy said lightly.

He tore his gaze from the screen to look over at her. The way she said the words indicated they spoke on a regular basis. Conversations that he would have loved to remember. "I really wish my memory would return."

"You seem to be working fine without it." She gestured to the computer. "Looks to me like you're making progress."

He wasn't referring to his job, but their relationship. They obviously knew each other, well enough to know where they lived. To get rides from each other. He assumed he and Cassidy were friends, which was nice. But the fact that she was the only team member he'd remembered last night, combined with his undeniable attraction to her, made him think he'd yearned for more.

A vain hope as a nerdy guy like him wouldn't have a chance with a beauty like Cassidy.

"I've found the virus and isolated it," he said, falling back on familiar turf. "Thankfully, it wasn't something too crazy. In another hour or so, we should be back online."

"Great." She rested a hand on his shoulder. "I knew you could do it."

He wanted to cover her hand with his, but he couldn't seem to move. He didn't want to make her feel uncomfortable, especially here in the precinct where they both worked. He forced himself to get back to the task at hand. Cassidy released him and moved away.

It was all he could do not to call her back.

Focus, he told himself sternly. *The entire precinct needs you to focus!*

He snacked on fruit-flavored candy as he worked. There was something familiar about being here. At some level, he was aware of the activity around him, but he was able to ignore the muted conversations. It wasn't until he'd successfully launched the departmental program that he realized how bad the pounding in his head had gotten.

"I'm in." His voice sounded odd to his ears, and he had to blink to bring Rhy's and Cassidy's faces into focus. "I need you both to try to log in now too. That will be the real test that we're back in business."

"Gabe, are you okay?" Cassidy's voice held concern. "You look pale."

He pressed the heels of his palms into his eyes. Maybe she'd been right about screen time not being good for concussions. His head hurt so badly he was tempted to crawl into one of the cots in the equipment room, pulling the covers over his head to sleep.

Wait a minute, how did he know there was a cot back there? The knowledge gave him hope his memory was returning. He lowered his hands to find Cassidy eyeing him with grave concern.

"I'm in," Rhy said with satisfaction. He grinned, his brown eyes full of relief and gratitude. "Incredible work, Gabe. You're amazing."

"Except that he looks like he might throw up," Cassidy said with a frown. "He needs rest, Rhy. He worked nonstop for two hours straight without his memory and battling a concussion."

Two hours? Gabe hadn't realized it had taken so long, but that explained his awful headache.

"Yes, of course." All hint of humor faded from Rhy's expression. "You may need to head over to the American Lodge for a while. You look like you could use some sleep."

The American Lodge sounded familiar, but he had no intention of leaving. "I'd rather stay here, close to the team."

Rhy frowned, glanced at Cass, and shrugged. "Okay, but you should get some rest. We'll wake you when it's time for lunch."

He wasn't hungry. Between the snacks and the headache, he felt sick to his stomach. "I'll get some rest," he agreed, hating to show weakness. "But there's more work to do. I need to figure out how these guys got in to activate the virus in the first place. And rebuild the firewall to prevent another attack." The more he considered the work ahead of him, the less he felt like sleeping. "Maybe I'll work for a little while longer . . ."

"No!" Cassidy's tone was vehement. "You need to rest

first. Pushing yourself could backfire, taking you out of commission even longer."

"I agree with Cassidy. You will go back and rest. That's an order," Rhy said sternly. "No argument. The alternative is to have Cassidy take you to the hospital."

"Okay, okay." Since Rhy's face was growing blurry, he figured an hour with his eyes closed would be good. Now that he'd gotten their operating system up and running, the weird sense of urgency had returned. Trying not to stress about what he was supposed to be doing, he pushed himself upright. Turning, he headed toward the equipment room. Cassidy kept pace beside him, as if worried he would fall over.

The room was well lit, but when he sank down onto the edge of the cot, Cassidy hit the light switch, plunging the room into darkness. The lack of light was a welcome relief. He stretched out on the cot, pulled the blanket up to his chin, and slowly relaxed.

"Rest well, Gabe," Cassidy whispered, before stepping back and closing the door behind her.

He found himself smiling at the image of Cassidy in his mind's eye as he drifted off to sleep.

"I DON'T LIKE THIS," Cassidy said when she joined Rhy in his office. As Gabe had contacted her, she'd gotten his case by default. "Clearly these incidents are related. It's likely the same person assaulted Gabe, ransacked his house, and sabotaged our system. What we need to know is why. What's the end goal?"

"I don't know," Rhy admitted. "Somehow, Gabe is at the

center of this, so keeping him close is a good plan. Other than that, we can only pray his memory returns."

"I have been praying for that since he contacted me last night." She had faith that God was watching over them, but it wasn't enough. "He's not working on anything for you, is he?"

"Nope." Rhy scowled. "It could be that whoever took his laptops from his place used them to send the virus through our system. Maybe they're just as computer savvy as he is."

She'd had the same thought. But there were points that didn't make sense. "Gabe was nearly killed while sitting in my kitchen, which begs the question, why had they let him live in the first place? Why hit him over the head and drop his body at the side of the road without making sure he was dead?" She hated thinking about how close Gabe had come to dying. "Unless they'd assumed he'd succumb to hypothermia last night, and when he didn't, they returned to finish the job."

"That's one possibility," Rhy agreed. "Or it could be that we have two different sets of assailants." His gaze rested on the computer atop his desk. "Makes me wonder if Gabe was using our system to do some sort of investigation of his own."

A chill snaked down her spine. Gabe could have easily used the police system to dig into something on his own time. They weren't the experts in that sort of thing. He was.

"We'll have to ask him about that when he wakes up." She hoped more of his memory would return by then too. Without that, they were searching for a faceless adversary while stumbling around in the dark.

Rhy eyed her thoughtfully. "I was hoping Gabe may have confided in you."

"Me?" Her eyes widened in surprise, and she felt herself flush. She and Gabe were friends, but she was friendly with the rest of the tactical team too. Why did Rhy think Gabe would talk to her over anyone else? "I, uh, no. He didn't."

"Hmm." Rhy frowned. "We need something to go on. I can call district five where Reed Carmichael works and see if their tech expert can get Gabe's cell phone records."

She knew Reed Carmichael was Rhy's brother-in-law, married to his younger sister Alanna who was an emergency department nurse at Trinity Medical Center. "Okay. Let me know when you get the data, I'll be happy to dig through to see who Gabe was talking to prior to his assault." She scowled and tried to think of another avenue to explore. "I could also check local pawn shops, see if any computer equipment has shown up."

Rhy nodded his approval as he reached for his phone. Leaving him to talk to his counterpart at the fifth district, she headed to an empty desk.

There were only two pawnshops in the city, unlike the dozens in Las Vegas, and of course neither of them reported getting any computer equipment in this morning. Both owners promised to call if that changed.

Sitting back in the chair, she stared off into the distance, wondering how the shooter had found Gabe at her place. An inside job? She scanned the precinct, which was mostly devoid of officers as they were all out on the street, but quickly dismissed the idea that anyone working here was responsible. As far as she knew, none of them had computer skills that were anywhere close to those possessed by Gabe. Besides, why hit him on the head, drop his body out in the middle of nowhere, and then shoot at him?

No, this wasn't police related. His personal electronics had been taken for a reason. Why, she had no idea.

But Gabe might know once his memory returned.

If his memory returned.

When her phone rang, she quickly grabbed it. Seeing an unknown number gave her pause. "Yes?"

There was a moment of silence, making the tiny hairs on the back of her neck lift in alarm.

"Who is this?" she demanded.

More silence. After another beat, she lowered the phone and looked at the screen. The caller had disconnected. After waiting a moment, she quickly redialed the unknown number.

But the call went straight to voice mail. A nonpersonalized voice mail.

"I'd like to chat," she said, feeling foolish at leaving a message for what could very well be a wrong number. "Call me back."

She set the phone on the desk next to her, practically willing it to ring. But the unknown caller didn't try again.

If Gabe were here, she'd ask him to track the number. But she wasn't sure how to do that. It occurred to her how much Rhy and the rest of them depended on Gabe's expertise. None of them could do even half of what he could.

And that wasn't good. All systems should have a level of redundancy.

"Cass?" Gabe emerged from the equipment room, his hair sticking up out of his head at odd angles. He looked different without his glasses, and she kinda missed watching him push them up on his nose. "We need to go back to my place."

"What?" She jumped to her feet. "Do you remember what happened?"

"Not really, but I think I left something in my house." His gaze implored her to go along with the plan. "Please. I need to check the freezer."

"The freezer?" She crossed over to put a hand on his arm. Clearly, his head injury had gotten worse. "You better sit down. I'll talk to Rhy. We need to take you to Trinity Medical Center right away."

"I don't need a hospital," Gabe said, shaking off her hand. His flash of annoyance was so unusual that she took a step back. "I'm not crazy or losing my mind. I woke up thinking I stuck something in the freezer for safety. You know, so that no one else would find it."

She eyed him warily, wondering if he really had used the freezer as a hiding place. But for what? Gabe's expertise was computers. "I don't think electronics work well at subzero temperatures."

"They don't," he agreed. "But I still need to check. Please, Cass. I need something to help jog my memory."

She glanced at Rhy's office, noticing he was on the phone again. Gabe's home in White Gull Bay wasn't that far from the precinct. She reluctantly nodded. "Okay, we'll go. But we need to get in and out of there relatively quickly."

"I can do that." He looked relieved that she'd given in. "Thank you. It's important." He grimaced, and added, "At least, it feels like it is."

She reached for her police-issue jacket that she'd tossed over the back of her chair. "We'll take the new undercover Jeep since Rhy doesn't want us driving our respective vehicles." She knew where the keys were located and headed over to grab them. "That should help provide some anonymity."

"Whatever works." He shrugged into his coat, wincing a

bit as if his head still hurt. "I appreciate you doing this for me."

She paused, noticing his choice of words. Remembering what Rhy had said about Gabe confiding in her, she asked, "Do you think this is something you've been working on by yourself? Outside of the precinct?"

"I, uh . . ." He looked surprised. "Maybe. Stealing my personal computers does lead to that conclusion, doesn't it?"

"Yes. Although that virus impacted the entire precinct."

"I know, and that worries me. I hate thinking I may have put everyone at risk by my actions." Gabe followed her outside into the cold December air. Dark clouds hung in the sky, but it wasn't snowing like it had been last night.

She unlocked the Jeep, then glanced at him. "You know that Rhy values your work. If you needed to investigate something, you could have discussed it with him. Maybe even gotten the rest of us involved."

"I know, and I wish now that I had." His brow furrowed. "At least then we'd have a clue as to what's going on."

Sensing there wasn't more to be gained from this line of questioning, she slid in behind the wheel of the Jeep and waited for Gabe to get settled beside her. She let the engine run for a moment to warm up, before backing out of the parking space and heading northeast to White Gull Bay.

"Have you heard from Zeke?" she asked.

"Who?" Gabe glanced at her in confusion.

She mentally kicked herself for bringing it up. "Never mind."

"No, really, I should know the people I work with." His gaze was earnest.

"I can't list them all, as you do work for every cop in the entire precinct. But those you work closest with are Rhy, whom you already met. He's our captain. Joe Kingsley is our lieutenant and Rhy's brother-in-law." She hoped rattling off the names wouldn't make Gabe feel worse about being unable to remember. "We have Steele Delaney, Brock Greer, Raelyn Washington, Grayson Clark, Roscoe Turner, Jina Robertson, Zeke Hawthorn, and Flynn Ryerson. Zeke was shot in the line of duty and has been off work since early October."

"So many," Gabe said. "It feels wrong not to be able to put faces with names." He glanced at her, and added, "Except for yours."

"It's fine; you'll remember soon." She did her best to sound positive. "Don't stress. You remembered putting something in the freezer, and that's a start."

"It's not even a clear memory," he groused. "Just an undeniable need to check the freezer for something that doesn't belong."

She still thought it was odd that he'd have put anything electronic in the freezer, but what did she know? She eyed the rearview mirror glad she hadn't noticed a tail. Then again, she hadn't noticed one last night either, and a shooter had still shown up at her condo. The thought made her realize she'd need to make arrangements to have the window repaired.

As she continued driving, another possibility struck her. "Does this have anything to do with your dad?"

"My dad? I don't think so." He looked thoughtful. "Last night you mentioned I inherited the house from him."

"Yes, he passed away two years ago, but you never explained in detail what happened. I always assumed he died of natural causes." She waved a hand. "Never mind, it was just a thought. The fact that you were attacked late at night and your home was ransacked has me thinking along the lines of this being a personal vendetta. But there was that virus at the station, too, so maybe not."

"Don't downplay your instincts, Cassidy." His tone was serious. "You're a good cop and should be asking questions. I just wish I had answers for you."

"Hopefully soon." She slowed as they approached White Gull Bay. "Look around, Gabe. This is your neighborhood. I need you to let me know if you notice anything suspicious."

"I'll try." He didn't sound confident, but she knew he wasn't giving himself enough credit. He had good observation skills. Maybe not like a cop, but better than the average citizen.

She found Gabe's place without difficulty. Cass decided to drive past the house first, without stopping, just to get a quick glimpse of the area. As she'd noticed last night, most of the houses around Gabe's were brightly decorated, which made it difficult to figure out if people were home.

"See anything unusual?" she asked. After going the length of three blocks, she turned to head back.

"No." He was still looking around with interest. "I don't remember growing up here. Makes me wonder when my dad bought the place."

Since she had no idea where he'd grown up, she didn't respond. She pulled over to the side of the road on the block behind Gabe's home. She killed the engine and turned to face him. "We're going to approach the place from the back. You don't have a fenced-in yard, so it shouldn't be difficult."

"Okay. Hopefully, the Landons won't call the police." He pushed open his car door and slid out.

The Landons? She found it fascinating the way some memories popped out of his mouth without his realizing it. Granted, she'd have preferred he remembered something better, like who had assaulted him and why, but she was hopeful this was a good sign.

She followed him along the side of the neighbor's driveway until they were cutting through the Landons' backyard. When they reached Gabe's property, she put a hand on his arm to stop him.

"Hold on," she said in a hushed tone. "Take a moment to look around. Do you see anything unusual?"

He frowned but did as she asked, carefully scanning the backyard. The snow from the night before had melted, and the only prints left behind were from small animals, rabbits or squirrels. "No. But you're making me nervous that I'm missing something important."

"You're not. I just want to be sure." She had thought that seeing his backyard in the daytime would bring more memories to the surface. "Looks like there's a keypad on the back door. Is it the same code as the garage?"

"I guess we'll find out. I'm not even sure how the code came to me last night, considering I wasn't even able to remember my last name." He took another moment to look around before crossing the backyard. The grass was still damp from the melted snow, and when she looked behind them, she noticed their footprints had left an obvious trail for anyone who cared to look.

Couldn't be helped. It was always a problem sneaking around in the winter. At least it was daytime, so they'd be able to see any potential threat clearly.

She watched as Gabe entered the key code. It took her a moment to realize the digits were her birthday. Had he done that on purpose? Or had he simply chosen the digits of 1014 randomly?

It was too late to ask, as he was already entering the house. She stayed close behind him, her hand resting on her weapon. Without her telling him to, he paused to listen.

Thankfully, there was nothing but silence.

Gabe moved quickly into the kitchen, straight for the freezer. The destruction of his home hadn't changed overnight; if anything, it looked worse in the daylight. Gabe opened the freezer and rummaged around.

Then he held up a small Styrofoam box. "Found it."

"Found what? Leftovers?"

"No, this." He reached for a knife, cut the tape that had held the two portions of the Styrofoam together, and pulled them apart. A small USB drive fell onto the kitchen counter.

"What's on it?" she asked, her pulse racing. This was exactly the clue they so desperately needed.

"I don't remember. But let's get it out of here so I can find out." His eyes gleamed with satisfaction as he dropped it into the front pocket of his jeans. "Whoever tossed the place didn't bother to look in the freezer."

Which meant he'd put it there specifically to hide it from view. Had Gabe anticipated someone would come after him? She was suddenly desperate to get far away from there.

"Follow me." She pulled her weapon and led the way out the back, retracing their steps. She half expected to be assaulted by a pair of gunmen, but they made it back to the undercover Jeep without difficulty.

"I'm glad you remembered stashing something in the freezer," she said, pulling away from the curb. "I forgot to mention that Rhy is getting your phone records too."

For a moment, Gabe looked panicked, but then he nodded. "That makes sense. I must have contacted someone to start this cascade of events."

"Exactly." She drove quickly, anxious to leave the city of White Gull Bay behind.

They had barely cleared the city limits when she noticed a black SUV coming up fast. Cass hit the gas, blowing past the stop sign and speeding through the intersection.

"What's going on?" Gabe asked.

Before she could answer, a crack of gunfire shattered the rear window.

"Get down!" Using every evasive driving maneuver she'd ever been taught, she wondered what on earth was on that USB drive that was worth killing for.

CHAPTER FIVE

Gabe huddled with his head down in the passenger seat as Cassidy wrenched the wheel from side to side, doing her best to shake off the shooter behind them. He hated feeling so helpless. The thumb drive seemed to be burning a hole in his pocket. He had to assume the same person who'd assaulted him had waited for him to arrive at his place to get the very item they'd been looking for.

But why? He didn't even know what was on the memory stick. He needed to get it plugged into a computer and soon.

"Call 911." Cassidy dropped the phone into the cupholder. "I should have taken the time to pair it with the Jeep's computer screen," she added half under her breath. Her gaze was laser focused on the road and cars around them. He understood she was desperately trying to get away from the shooter while keeping the public safe.

No easy task.

He did as she asked, lifting his head enough to give the dispatcher a location. They were already leaving White

Gull Bay, though, so he wasn't sure which district would even respond.

"We're passing Duran Street heading south on Lakeshore Drive," he said, as they paralleled the Lake Michigan shoreline. The lake was quiet and beautiful during wintertime.

"I've dispatched officers to your location," the woman said calmly. "Please stay on the line."

He was about to set the phone on speaker when their car abruptly slowed. He glanced at Cass who looked grim.

"Gas tank is hit; we'll need to bail."

Bail? As in leave the car? He swallowed hard. She was the expert here, not him. "Okay. I'm ready."

She made a right turn, then hit the brakes. "Hurry," she said, pushing her driver's side door open.

He followed suit, jumping out of the passenger seat. He followed Cassidy as she jogged up the road, then cut through a private residence. Trusting her instincts, he stayed close, despite his discomfort at invading people's privacy by running through their yards.

Thankfully, no one seemed to notice as they darted through one backyard and the next. Cassidy made what appeared to be totally random turns, but he sensed she had a plan. He kept pace beside her, breathing heavily from the exertion. The pain in his head thumped along with the beat of his heart, making it hard to concentrate on staying upright and following Cass.

He knew without being told that this type of thing was not something he'd done on a regular basis. If ever. Cassidy and Rhy had mentioned he was their tech specialist, and there was no denying he was more comfortable behind a desk.

Finally, Cassidy crouched near a large tree in the backyard of a house that was large and expensive looking. He wasn't sure if there were people inside or not, but he hoped for the latter as he dropped beside her. For a moment, he closed his eyes, grateful for the opportunity to catch his breath. Then he looked around, trying to gauge where they were. Somewhere on the east side, but how far had they gone on foot?

He had no idea.

"Are you okay?" Her eyes betrayed her concern.

"Yeah." He didn't want to let her know how badly his head hurt. "I can keep up."

She gestured to the phone he still held in his hand. "Smart move to bring the phone."

He grimaced. There had been nothing brilliant about his actions; he hadn't even realized he'd hung onto it. He passed it to her. "Take it. I suspect we're going to need it."

She accepted the phone and slipped it into the back pocket of her jeans. "We need to keep moving. It's the middle of the day. Someone is bound to see us skulking through backyards."

"Okay." He was in no position to argue. "Shouldn't we call Rhy?"

"Soon. Once we're in a public place where we can wait for a ride." She gestured behind them. "We're not far enough away from the Jeep. We've only gone a little over a mile."

Seriously? It had seemed like far more. "I'll keep up," he repeated to reassure her. "I won't hold you back."

She flashed a quick smile, which resonated deep within despite their dire circumstances. He must have a screw loose because he should be more concerned with staying alive than focusing on how beautiful Cassidy was. "You're doing great, Gabe. We'll get through this." She cast a sweeping glance around their current location, then added, "Let's go."

With a muffled groan, he stood and followed her through the next backyard until they were on a residential street. She set a brisk pace, and he was glad he hadn't lied about being able to keep up. His long stride helped, and the exertion of covering ground quickly kept the winter chill at bay.

Soon they were on busier streets, and he noticed they were approaching one of the university buildings. "We're close to the University of Milwaukee," he said, surprised he recognized it.

"Yes." She arched a brow. "I attended college here to major in criminal justice, but you went to Madison."

He tried to remember attending the University of Madison but couldn't. Not that it mattered. He'd rather remember if he was investigating some case that had gotten him assaulted and dumped in the middle of nowhere.

"That restaurant there should work," Cassidy said in a low voice. "We'll call Rhy and see if someone can head out to pick us up."

The scent of food made him feel hungry. He doubted they'd sticking around, though, so he didn't say anything.

A blessed warmth washed over them as they stepped inside. "Table for two, please," Cassidy said.

They were soon seated in a booth lining a wall of windows overlooking the street. There were many pedestrians milling about, and he realized that most of them were students. This was likely the week of final exams, bringing an end to the fall semester.

"What can I get you to drink?" a perky server asked.

"Hot chocolate," Cassidy said without hesitation.

"Me too, thanks." He waited for the young woman to leave, before asking, "Are you going to call Rhy?"

"Yes." She sat back in her seat with a sigh. "He won't be happy about this. Maybe we should eat lunch first, as long as we're here."

"That's fine with me." He patted his pocket. "Although I am anxious to look at this external drive."

"Me too." Her phone buzzed, and when she pulled it out, she turned to show him Rhy's name on the screen. "Time's up," she said, before lifting the phone to her ear. "Hey, Rhy."

He knew she couldn't put the call on speaker as they were in a public place, so he quickly jumped out of his seat to scoot in beside her. He placed his ear near hers so he could listen in.

"Cassidy?" Rhy asked. "What's this about reports of gunfire in White Gull Bay? Is that where you and Gabe are?"

"Yes, sir," she said. "We were in White Gull Bay. Shortly after leaving Gabe's residence, gunfire shattered the rear window of the Jeep, but we're okay." She hesitated, then said, "Unfortunately, one of the bullets hit the gas tank. We had to abandon the Jeep and escape on foot. We're near the UWM campus now, at a restaurant."

There was a slight pause, before Rhy said, "I'm glad you're both not hurt. I'll take care of getting the Jeep towed. I'm more concerned with how you were found in the first place. The Jeep isn't registered in either of your names."

"I've been thinking about that," Cassidy admitted. "I have to assume that whoever is running this operation may have had someone stationed near Gabe's house on the chance we'd return. Either that or we were followed from the precinct. I didn't notice a tail but could have missed one."

"I doubt you'd have missed a tail," Rhy said. Gabe was glad their boss didn't seem too upset over the damaged Jeep. "Care to fill me in on what made you head out to Gabe's house in the first place?"

"Gabe remembered hiding something in his freezer," Cassidy explained. "You were on the phone, or I would have let you know where we were going. Sorry about that. But the good news is that we found a USB drive stored in Styrofoam in Gabe's freezer."

"A USB drive?" Rhy sounded surprised. "What's on it?"

"We don't know yet." Cassidy turned her head slightly to glance at him. "I'm hoping someone can drive out to pick us up so that we can get back to the precinct to find out."

"Okay, I'll see if Steele or Raelyn can swing by," Rhy said. "I'm texting them both now. That was only one reason I called. There's been a recent development I thought you should be aware of."

Gabe's heart thudded as a strange sense of apprehension washed over him.

"What?" Cassidy asked.

"Gabe's seventeen-year-old half brother, Travis McCord, went missing yesterday," Rhy said. "His mother just called asking for Gabe. She was hoping Gabe may have heard from him or could track him down using his phone. Apparently, she tried the find my phone app but without success."

Half brother? Shocked by the news, he tried to remember a half brother named Travis. But the gray mist in his mind remained unyielding.

Were he and Travis close? He had no idea.

Yet he knew with sick certainty that whatever had

happened to Travis must be linked to the attack on him. And he desperately needed to remember what had transpired to begin this horrifying cascade of events.

Before something terrible happened to Travis.

"I DIDN'T REALIZE Gabe had a half brother," Cassidy said, feeling Gabe stiffen beside her. She had a bad feeling Gabe didn't remember him either. She thought it was odd because she had told him a few things about her stepsiblings who were about her same age, twenty-seven and twenty-nine, respectively. They were gamers like Gabe, which was why she'd mentioned them. She didn't see Ben and Brian as often as she probably should, but from what she gathered, Gabe was estranged from his half brother. "As soon as we get back to the precinct, Gabe can get to work on tracking him."

"We have to hurry," Gabe hissed. "Tell Rhy to send someone to get us ASAP."

Cassidy understood his concern. "Glad you heard back from Steele. Have him meet us out front. Thanks, Rhy." She lowered the phone, scooting over to put some room between herself and Gabe. "I'm sorry about your half brother, but I'm sure you'll find him."

"I can't remember him." Gabe thrust his fingers through his brown hair. "How is it possible I don't remember my own half brother?"

"Gabe." She put a hand on his arm. "You told me your mother traded up. Left your father for a hot-shot lawyer. I didn't get the sense that you and your mother remained close. Which means you may not have spent much time with Travis. Plus, there is a significant age gap between you."

A mixture of relief and frustration played across his features. "Even if we're not close, I feel responsible for his disappearance. Like maybe I had something to do with it."

Cass nodded as that possibility had occurred to her too. "Do you think it's possible you were heading out to meet with Travis last night?"

Gabe's eyes widened in surprise. "I don't know, maybe. Although I doubt Travis would have hit me over the head and left me at the side of the road."

"It's best to keep an open mind," she said gently. Then she sat back as their server returned with their hot chocolates.

"Are you ready to order?" she asked.

"No, sorry. Change in plans," Cassidy said. "Please bring our bill."

The server looked disappointed, shrugged, and left. Two minutes later, she set their bill on the table. "Have a nice day," she said, without meaning it.

"I can pay," Gabe offered.

"Let me. We may need your funds later." Cassidy glanced at the total and pulled cash from her pocket. She added a substantial tip to smooth things over, then reached for her hot chocolate. "We have at least ten minutes before Steele will get here."

Gabe cradled the mug without drinking. "I can't stand it," he whispered. "All along I've felt this strange sense of urgency, as if there's something very important that I need to do." He shook his head and lifted his gaze to hers. "Maybe that important task is to find Travis. What if he's in trouble? Maybe he called and asked for help. I could have gone to the meeting place because he asked me to, but the attackers got there first. They attacked me, leaving me there and took off with Travis as their hostage."

She preferred cold, hard facts over speculation, but obviously theories were all they had. His proposal was possible, among dozens of others. "Try not to think the worst." She forced a reassuring smile. "I'm sure the USB drive will provide answers."

"I pray you're right," Gabe said. "Because the not remembering is killing me. If something bad happens to Travis . . ."

"It won't be your fault," she said, placing a hand on his arm. "You're doing the best you can, Gabe. Let's take this one step at a time. The last time we spoke, you mentioned your mother lived in Madison."

"You know more than I do." A hint of bitterness laced his tone. "I have no idea where she lives."

"But the way you were found near the Wildflower Motel indicates you may have headed out to a neutral location to meet with Travis. Or someone else who claimed to know information about him."

Gabe pushed his hot chocolate aside without tasting it. "I can't just sit here. Let's head outside to wait."

Knowing that the case had turned personal—more so than a random attack at the side of the road—she nodded. Taking another long sip of her hot chocolate, she followed Gabe out of the booth toward the front door. Before he could step outside, she snagged his arm, holding him back.

He shot her an impatient glance that was so unlike the Gabe she knew that she paused.

"I just need you to stay back until I can make sure it's safe," she explained. "We're only a few miles from the damaged Jeep. The gunmen could still be searching for us."

He held her gaze for a long moment before stepping back.

She pushed the door open and stepped into the cold, quickly scanning the area. There were so many people that it would be nearly impossible to spot a shooter. Yet she felt compelled to try.

A group of four came toward her, obviously intending to eat lunch. She stepped aside, then gestured for Gabe to come out and join her. His height made him stand out, not to mention impossible for her shorter frame to adequately provide cover for him, so she tugged him over to the side, praying the shooter was long gone.

"I hope Steele gets here soon," Gabe muttered. "It seems to be getting colder."

He was right. Rather than warming up as the afternoon approached, the wind had shifted coming in from the north. She tucked her chin into her coat, still keeping a wary eye out for danger.

"There he is," she said in relief, recognizing Steele's SUV. Her fellow teammate pulled up directly in front of the door. She hurried forward, taking the front passenger seat out of habit, leaving Gabe to crawl into the back. "Thanks for coming," she said.

"Anytime," Steele said, glancing back at Gabe. "I heard you can't remember anything prior to being attacked and left at the side of the road."

"Yeah, it's not good." Gabe sounded more dejected than ever. "I need everyone to pray that my memory returns as soon as possible."

She and Steele exchanged surprised looks, as Gabe had never mentioned praying before. "I have been," she said. "And I know the others are keeping you in their prayers too."

"They need to include Travis as well," Gabe said wearily. "The half brother I can't remember."

She noticed Steele's eyes widen in surprise and quickly filled him in on the latest.

"I agree the assault against Gabe must be related to his missing half brother," Steele said. "Hopefully that USB drive you found in the freezer will provide answers."

"It better," Gabe said. "Otherwise, I don't know where we should even start to find Travis."

She exchanged another concerned glance with Steele. Gabe sounded more upset than ever, and she couldn't come up with any way to reassure him. She turned in her seat to face him. "Why wouldn't your mother be able to use the find my phone app to locate Travis? I mean, from a technical perspective. Does that mean his phone is off or simply out of range?"

"Off or damaged," Gabe said without hesitation. "The newer phones can be tracked all the way across the globe."

"Really?" She gaped. "How is that possible?"

Gabe shrugged. "The new phones have the same technology that is used in air tags. You know, to track your luggage while traveling."

"That's interesting," she said in awe. "I hadn't realized the technology was that good."

"Yeah." He grimaced. "In this case, based on the way my house was searched and the TV screen damaged, it's likely Travis's phone is in a similar condition. Damaged to the point we can't use it to find him."

She silently agreed with Gabe's assessment. Steele made good time in returning to the precinct. When Steele pulled into a parking spot in the rear lot, Gabe bolted from the car before it had come to a complete stop.

Shooting an apologetic glance at Steele, she hurried to catch up.

A man on a mission, Gabe strode purposefully toward the closest laptop computer even as he pulled the USB drive from his pocket. She found herself holding her breath as Gabe powered up the device, then logged into the system.

Once he was in, he slid the USB drive into an opening along the side of the laptop. He double-clicked the icon. Over his shoulder, she could see there was only one file on the drive. Somehow, she'd expected more.

Like maybe pictures or a video. Instead, what bloomed on the screen was nothing but gibberish.

Her hope plummeted. "The file is corrupted."

"No, I don't think so." Gabe stared intently at the screen, slowly scrolling down to the bottom of the page. "It's computer code of some sort."

"Computer code may as well be gibberish," she said, as Steele came up to stand beside them. "Unless you know what it means?"

"I'm not sure." Gabe scowled as he returned to the top of the document. "It must be the code to some program."

"Some program?" Steele echoed. "But you don't know which one?"

"Not yet." Gabe finally turned to look up at her. "It's going to take some time for me to figure out what this code belongs to. Time we don't have." His expression looked tortured. "We need to try to find Travis. And I don't think identifying what this code is related to won't help us with that."

She hid her disappointment. The code on this USB drive had to be the reason they'd taken gunfire. Which meant it must be important.

But without Gabe's memory, they were still in the dark as to what was really going on.

"Why don't you see if you can find the last cell tower your half brother's phone pinged from?" Steele suggested. "That will give us a starting point."

"Good call." Gabe looked relieved to have a job to do. He turned back to the computer. As she watched, he took a moment to attach the mystery computer code to an email and send it off to the entire team. A smart move since now they all had ready access to the information.

No clue how to interpret it, but the ability to open it was half the battle.

Gabe pulled up a new program on his computer and began working the keyboard. It was a relief to know he'd retained basic knowledge of how to do these sorts of tasks since most of them were beyond the team's abilities.

It gave her hope that he'd be able to unlock the mystery code very soon.

"Okay, I have the program up and running," Gabe said. "But I need the phone number."

"I have it here," Rhy said, crossing the room toward them waving a blue sticky note. "Your mother gave it to me."

Gabe took the note and typed in the number. After a few minutes, he said, "Got it. The phone pinged last off this tower." He pointed to the screen. "And that call was made at three minutes past nine last night."

"Looks like the tower is about two miles from the Wild-flower Motel," she said, reading the map over Gabe's shoulder. A chill snaked down her spine. "That makes me think you and Travis were together at the time."

"Together or Travis asked me to meet him there," Gabe said. "I am not sure why I didn't drive my car, though. It seems strange that I would have taken a rideshare all that way."

"We should have your phone records soon," Rhy said. "That will confirm your communication with your half brother."

"And if you took a rideshare," she added. "It could be that someone showed up at your house and demanded you go with them to meet Travis."

There was a long silence as they pondered that possibility. Then Gabe abruptly pushed away from the desk. "We need to go back to the area where I woke up. Maybe the assailants left something behind."

Cass glanced questioningly at Rhy and Steele. She'd damaged the undercover Jeep and didn't have a car.

Steele nodded. "I'll drive."

"Thanks." She caught up to Gabe who was halfway to the door. Their tech analyst was always focused when it came to his work, but this single-minded determination was off the charts.

The trip out to the Wildflower Motel didn't take long as Steele flicked on his red and blue lights, forcing cars to move out of their way. She gave him a sidelong glance.

"Hey, we're heading to a crime scene," Steele said defensively.

"One that's not in our jurisdiction," she felt compelled to point out. "But hey, I'm not arguing."

"Faster," Gabe said from the back seat. "I wish I'd have thought of coming back here last night."

She felt guilty over that too, but at the time they hadn't known about the break-in at Gabe's home, or his missing half brother. "I'm sorry. I hope there's still some evidence left behind."

"It's not your fault," Gabe said. "I'm the one who can't remember anything useful."

As they approached the off-ramp, Gabe leaned forward. "Head left, Steele. Maybe two miles down the road."

Steele followed his directions.

"Here, pull over here," Gabe said. "I was in that field."

The area was familiar; several of the team members had rendezvoused nearby several months ago. Gabe bolted from the car. She and Steele quickly followed.

"Spread out," Steele said. "We'll cover more ground that way."

She nodded in agreement. Several areas of the ground were trampled by footprints, but none that could be isolated enough to be of use.

Then she heard an agonized cry. Spinning toward Gabe, she reached for her weapon, half expecting to see an attacker.

Instead, Gabe was kneeling on the ground, his expression grim. She rushed over to see the remains of a destroyed phone. By his despair, she knew it was likely Travis's.

Their only connection to the missing teenager.

CHAPTER SIX

Seeing the smashed phone gutted him. The phone case featured the latest video game called Sorcerer's Sword, and he instinctively knew it had belonged to Travis.

Gabe abruptly surged to his feet, raking his gaze around the area. "We need to look for him."

"Easy," Cassidy murmured, putting a hand on his arm. "Let us do that. You stay back out of the way."

A flash of anger hit hard. "This is about me," he said sharply. "I don't know how or why, but this is about me!"

Cassidy's blue eyes widened in surprise at his vehemence. "I know that, Gabe. We're here to find out what happened. But if a crime has been committed, we can't trample the crime scene more than we already have."

A crime had taken place, the lump on the back of his head was proof of that. But he understood what she meant. It wasn't easy to bite back his frustration, but he managed a curt nod. "Okay. You and Steele spread out to see what you find." He gestured to the damaged phone. "And this should be taken in as evidence."

"I'm on it," Steele said, pulling a bag from his coat

pocket. Turning the bag inside out, he scooped up the phone remnants. Gabe swallowed hard as he wondered what had taken place. Had Travis been kidnapped? And if so, why?

He watched as Steele and Cass spread out to examine the area. The way they swept their gazes over the ground, as if searching for the smallest indication of a crime, gave him hope. If clues had been left behind, he trusted the officers would find them.

"There's some blood here," Cassidy called.

He turned, then grimaced. "It's probably mine. I think that was where I was when I woke up and realized I'd been attacked."

"Okay, we can check it to make sure." She glanced at Steele. "You have evidence markers in the SUV?"

"I'll grab them." Steele strode to the SUV, opened the back, and removed a handful of neon yellow markers. "We'll need the crime scene techs out here too."

It was on the tip of his tongue to offer to make the call, then he remembered he didn't have a phone. He made a mental note to stop on the way back to the precinct to get a replacement. Something he should have done earlier.

He tried not to show his impatience as Cass and Steele continued to comb the area. After a solid twenty minutes, they returned to where he stood waiting.

"I didn't find anything else, did you?" Cassidy asked Steele.

"Nope. I guess that's good news," Steele said with a shrug. "If the blood we found belongs to Gabe, it appears as if Travis wasn't hurt here."

"Maybe he was hurt somewhere else," Gabe said, unable to let it go. "I could have come here to meet with Travis only to realize someone else had his phone."

"That is possible," Cassidy said. "But so are lots of other theories. We'll get your phone records and Travis's as well. That should reveal a significant part of the story."

"Try not to focus on the worst-case scenarios," Steele said, obviously sensing his anger and frustration. "Getting mad won't help. We need to deal with the evidence as it's presented to us."

"I'll try," he said grudgingly. "But Travis is just a kid. I can't stand the idea of something bad happening to him."

He noticed how Steele and Cassidy exchanged a quick, grim expression and knew they were worried about Travis as well.

"How soon will the crime scene techs get here?" He was suddenly anxious to get to the closest store. "I need to buy a replacement phone. If I can remember my password, I'll have access to my text and phone messages."

"Do you think you can remember it?" Steele asked with a frown.

"I don't know. I was able to access my work computer without really thinking about it." He suspected that was mostly because it was a task he did every single day. "I'm hoping the same is true for my phone."

"Good idea," Cassidy said, looking encouraged. "The way you knew the code to your garage door makes me think you can do the same with your phone. We'll head out as soon as the crime scene techs arrive."

"Take my car," Steele suggested, tossing his key fob to Cass. "I'll wait here for them. You and Gabe can buy the phone, then swing back to pick me up."

"Thank you, Steele," he said, meaning it. The way the team was rallying around him was humbling. "I appreciate you and the others more than you know."

"Hey, you've been there to back us up when we were in

tough situations." Steele waved a hand. "This is the least we can do in return."

"Steele is right, you've been a rock for the team." Cass favored him with a sweet smile. One that made him wish he had the right to kiss her. "We won't stop until we get to the bottom of this."

He was too choked up to respond, so he turned and headed for Steele's SUV. When they were back on the highway, his thoughts went back to Travis. "I need a picture of my half brother," he said. "It's bugging me that I can't remember him."

"We'll find one," Cassidy assured him. "But you may have one on your phone."

"I hope so." He fell silent, the image of the Sorcerer's Sword video game on Travis's phone nagging at him. He'd recognized it as the new game that had recently hit the market. It was being touted as the hottest Christmas gift for gamers, and the software was already flying off the shelves.

But there was a way to get the software without going to the store to buy it. Wasn't there? From gaming systems maybe? He pressed his fingertips to his temples as he struggled to remember.

"Hey, are you okay?" Cassidy put a hand on his knee. "Don't stress, Gabe. We're going to find him."

He didn't have the heart to tell her he was thinking about a stupid video game rather than his half brother. He tried to smile and covered her hand with his. "I know. I trust you, Cass."

"I'm glad." Her soft husky voice sent ripples of awareness coursing over him. Talk about the wrong time, wrong place, and wrong situation. "And you should trust in God too. He will guide us to the truth."

He nodded, realizing faith was a core value for Cassidy.

And for him too? Maybe, although he didn't have a clear memory of attending church. Still, he needed all the help he could get. "I will put my trust in God. But to be honest, I have just as much faith in you, Rhy, the entire tactical team. I hope that's not the wrong answer."

"It's not." Her smile brightened, and they held hands until the familiar big box store came into view.

"There," he said, waving at it. "That will work."

Cass exited the interstate and headed for the store. When they walked in, he couldn't help but feel as if the place was familiar. Had he worked in a place like this while attending college? Or was it just that he tended to like video games and electronics? Either way, he quickly found the phone section.

"I'll take this one," he said without looking around at the others.

The clerk widened his eyes and nodded. "Good choice. I'll ring you up over here."

That's when he remembered he only had the cash he'd found in his dresser drawer. He pulled it from his pocket and counted the bills.

"Better if I put the phone on my credit card," Cassidy said, adding two more disposable phones to their purchases. "These will increase the cost anyway. And I don't want to waste our cash in case we need it later."

He bit his lip, nodded, and stuffed the money back into his pocket. "Okay, but I promise I'll pay you back."

"I'm not worried," Cass assured him. "We work together, remember? It's not like you can hide from me."

That made him smile, despite the circumstances. It didn't feel good to allow Cass to pay for his phone, but as soon as he had the device, he stared at the screen, willing his password to come back to him.

It didn't.

He hesitated, instinctively knowing he wouldn't have used the same password for his work computer on his personal device.

"Give it time," Cassidy said as they headed back outside to Steele's SUV. "It will come to you."

Would it? Panic swelled in his chest, and he did his best to wrestle it back. Some of his memories had returned, mostly when he wasn't expecting them. He closed his eyes and cleared his mind. He envisioned himself at home, sitting in the living room that had not been ransacked and trashed.

Cassha$myheart.

His eyelids flew open, and he quickly picked up the phone. He quickly accessed the settings and typed in the password that had flashed in his mind.

It worked!

"I'm in," he said excitedly for Cassidy's benefit. "I remembered the password."

"Check your recent messages," she urged.

He was already thumbing the home screen to bring them up. But there were none. Not a single message.

That couldn't be right. He tried again, then went to his recent calls. There were none listed there either. A flash of panic surged again as he tried various ways to retrieve his messages and other personal data. But there was nothing. Not even any photos had been stored in the cloud.

Which meant only one thing. His phone had been wiped clean.

CASSIDY GLANCED AT Gabe with concern. "What's wrong?"

He lifted his tortured gaze to hers. "Somehow, my personal information on my phone has been sanitized."

She frowned. "Sanitized meaning . . . what?"

"It's all gone." He sounded so dejected her heart ached for him. "Wiped clean."

She had no idea how someone could even do that. "Maybe you typed in the wrong password and that's why none of your data is in there."

He slowly shook his head. "That's not it. I'm sure it's the right password."

"I don't understand," she said after a long minute. "How can something like that even happen?"

"It's not by accident," Gabe said somberly. "It was done on purpose. Either by me or the bad guys."

She tried to follow his logic. "So the bad guys assaulted you, took your phone, and wiped it clean? You have tech savvy bad guys after you?"

He turned to look at her. "You're onto something, Cass. The bad guys must have tech skills. They stole my computers, my phone, and my gaming system. They smashed my TV screen for good measure."

"Okay, but why?" She still didn't understand. "Why would they do all of that?"

"I don't know. But I'm very much afraid Travis is in the middle of this in some way. The case on his phone featured the latest video game, so he's a techy too."

That made sense. To a point. "I guess I'm not seeing how a computer game can be dangerous."

"I'm not sure this is about the game itself. It could be more about proprietary information. Like maybe someone is trying to steal the video game source code for some reason. To pirate it or to sabotage it."

She took the Wildflower Motel exit. This was so far outside her area of expertise she felt a headache coming on just thinking about it. "I think we need to eat lunch," she said. "My brain needs protein."

He looked impatient. "We don't have time for that. We need to find Travis."

"And we can't do that if we don't take care of ourselves." She glanced at him with exasperation as she pulled off at the side of the road behind the large crime scene tech van. "You love to eat, Gabe. You're always snacking, even while working. Your famous line is that you need food to think clearly."

His brown eyes widened in surprise. Then he finally nodded. "Okay, you're right. If I'm being honest, my stomach is growling. We can eat while we discuss our next steps."

"Good." She glanced over as Steele jogged up to the car. "Are you interested in lunch?"

"Very," Steele said with a grin. He slid into the back seat. "Did you find anything useful from the phone?"

Gabe sighed and filled Steele in on the fact that the phone storage had been wiped clean. She caught Steele's gaze in the rearview and shrugged. She didn't have anything to add. The whole thing was a mystery that only Gabe could solve.

And his memory loss was the biggest hurdle holding them back.

"Good idea to get disposable phones too," Steele said, rummaging through the bag.

"I know the routine," she said dryly. She headed to a restaurant that wasn't too far from the big box store where they'd picked up Gabe's phone. Ten minutes later, they were seated in a booth with menus in hand.

"What would you like to drink?" their server asked.

"Hot chocolate," she and Gabe answered at the same time.

"Coffee for me," Steele said, shaking his head. "You guys and your chocolate."

She shrugged and scanned the menu. After their server returned with their hot drinks, she took their order and hurried off.

"I spoke to Rhy while I was waiting," Steele said, cupping his hands around his coffee mug for warmth. He was clearly more chilled as he'd been standing around outside the entire time she and Gabe were gone. Steele glanced at Gabe. "He sent Roscoe's cousin Cameron to interview your mom and her husband to get more information regarding the last time they've seen or spoken to Travis."

"That's good," Cass said. "Maybe we can narrow down the timeline of when he went missing."

"I hope so." Gabe frowned. "I really need a few pictures. It's sad, but I can't bring forth any clear memories of my own mother."

She winced, putting a hand on his arm. They were seated side by side in the booth, with Steele across from them. "You weren't close to your mom, Gabe. You told me she divorced your father to marry a rich lawyer." She paused, then added, "A criminal defense lawyer, which your father viewed as a slap in the face."

"My dad was an MPD detective," Gabe said hotly. "Of course, it was a slap in the face."

"See? You remembered your dad because you were close to him. You joined the police department as a civilian but have dedicated your life to supporting cops. Like us," she said, gesturing to herself and Steele. "So don't be upset that you can't remember your mother."

"I guess." Gabe sipped his hot chocolate. "But she's still my mother."

"Hang on, I think I found a photograph of her," Steele said, working his phone. Then he turned the device so Gabe could see the screen. "Does this help?"

She leaned closer to Gabe as he took the phone. Steele had used his fake social media profile to find Shelia McCord. The woman on the screen was pretty, but her smile came across as more calculating than nice as she stood next to a slightly overweight man with gray hair at his temples.

"Yeah, that's her." Gabe said. "I remember her now. She married Paul McCord, and they had Travis within one year after their wedding." He handed the phone back to Steele. "Odd that I don't have childhood memories to go along with this."

"I believe you lived with your dad," Cass said. "At least, that's the way you made it sound."

"That solves one mystery," Gabe muttered. "She gave me up in favor of a life of luxury."

She shot a helpless glance at Steele, unsure of how to answer.

"Her loss, Gabe," Steele said. "And God expects us to forgive those who trespass against us. Holding a grudge hurts you, not her."

"That's true," Cassidy agreed. "Besides, who did she come to when she needed help?"

"Yeah, I'll do my best," Gabe said. But she wasn't sure if he meant in finding Travis or in forgiving his mother.

Maybe both.

"Can you find a picture of Travis?" Gabe asked.

"Hang on." Steele scrolled through the site, then nodded. "Here's one."

Gabe took the phone. On the screen was a skinny, tall teenager with long brown hair, the same brown eyes as Gabe, and wearing clothes that looked like they were from a rummage sale but had likely been purchased with the rips and holes in them. To her mind, he looked like a younger, scruffier version of Gabe.

"He looks familiar," Gabe said. "But I can't picture us being together."

She shrugged. "Maybe you mostly text each other. He lives in Madison, after all."

"True." Gabe passed the phone back to Steele again. "Thanks. I appreciate the assistance."

"Anytime." Steele assured him.

Their meals arrived, and her stomach grumbled so loudly at the enticing scent of her grilled chicken sandwich and cream of mushroom soup that Steele and Gabe snickered.

She shrugged off the embarrassment. She glanced at Steele, who took the lead in saying grace.

"Dear Lord Jesus, we thank You for this food, and we ask that You keep Travis and all of us looking for him safe in Your care. Amen."

"Amen," she and Gabe echoed.

They ate in silence for a few minutes. Even Gabe seemed to be enjoying his meal, despite his missing half brother.

Finding Travis's destroyed phone had been a setback, but she knew it was entirely possible that Travis had done the deed himself. To cover his tracks in some way. Not that Travis had looked capable of slamming Gabe in the head and leaving him along the deserted road, but maybe someone Travis had teamed up with.

Was this really related to a video game? Despite Gabe's comments about the possibility, she found it hard to believe. Corporate espionage, maybe. One company stealing technology from another.

But if that was the case, why on earth would a kid like Travis be involved?

"I should talk to my mom," Gabe said, breaking the silence. "I know Cameron is interviewing her, but I should talk to her too."

She shrugged. "That's fine with me. But let's wait until we get back to the precinct. I'm sure Rhy has her number. And it's best to use a different phone other than yours."

"Does the fact that your phone was wiped mean that we won't get anything from your phone records?" Steele asked.

Gabe grimaced. "Probably. It depends on when the sanitization happened, but I'm sure that was last night."

Steele sighed. "That's a bummer."

Gabe finished his meal and pushed his plate aside. "Here are the next steps we should take. First, I reach out to my mom to see what she knows. It's possible she'll tell me something she might hold back from the police. Especially if she thinks Travis might get in trouble for whatever he's been doing." He drummed his fingers on the table. "I think the best thing I can do to get to the bottom of this is to focus on the data we recovered from the USB drive I hid in my freezer. I must have put it there for a good reason."

"That sounds like a plan." She finished her sandwich and soup, feeling better to have something in her stomach. "It seems logical that the bad guys tossed your place to get that information."

"I agree." Steele pulled out his wallet and signaled for

the bill. "Meanwhile, we can ask for Travis's phone records. Maybe they haven't been wiped clean."

"I think Rhy may have already asked for them," Cassidy said. "That's protocol when investigating a missing person."

"Let's get back to the precinct, then," Gabe said, waving a hand impatiently. "I want to get started on that data."

He was acting like his usual self, so much so that she had to remind herself that his memory hadn't fully recovered.

They had to wait for their server to return. She finally arrived with the bill, looking harried. "I hope everything was good?"

"Great, thanks." Gabe barely spared her a glance, making it clear he wanted to get out of there.

Steele paid in cash, leaving a generous tip. Cassidy was the last to get out of the booth, following both men as they made their way outside.

By force of habit, Steele paused at the doorway, peering through the glass before pushing the door open. Gabe stood back to allow her to go next. She gave him a reassuring smile as she headed out to the SUV.

"I'll take the keys," Steele said with a grin. "Not that you're a bad driver or anything," he hastily added. "But it is my vehicle."

"Whatever." She tossed them to him. To her surprise, Gabe climbed into the back seat, leaving her the front.

A minute later, they were back on the road, heading east toward Milwaukee. She wondered again if the meeting point near the Wildflower Motel was viewed as some sort of halfway point between Gabe's home in White Gull Bay and Travis's house in Madison.

"Uh, Cass?" Tension lined Steele's tone as he abruptly

hit the gas. He then flicked the switch to activate the red and blue light bar on top. "We have company."

"What?" She turned in her seat in time to see a black SUV coming up hot behind them. Even with Steele using lights, they were closing the distance. "Gabe, get down!"

He ducked just as the sharp report of gunfire echoed around them. Steele wrenched the wheel to the left, abruptly changing lanes, but she thought she heard a metallic ping as one of the bullets struck the vehicle.

Thankfully, the rear window was still intact. She sniffed the air but didn't detect the scent of gas either. Steele had the advantage, as cars moved out of his way. But that only meant the black SUV behind them had a clear path to follow as well.

"Call 911," Steele shouted. She quickly found her phone, hoping the state patrol was stationed nearby.

Steele jerked the wheel again, moving to the right this time, crossing three lanes of traffic in time to exit the interstate. It was a smart decision, and a quick glance confirmed the black SUV had not been able to mirror their movement.

They were safe for now.

But whoever these bad guys were, they had every intention of eliminating Gabe.

Permanently.

CHAPTER SEVEN

This was all his fault. Gabe hated knowing Cassidy and Steele were in danger because of him. And even though Steele had claimed they'd lost the gunmen, he'd turned in his seat to stare out the back window, expecting them to materialize at any moment.

As if they had some sort of superhuman powers.

"Gabe, is it possible they can track your new phone?" Cassidy asked, diverting his attention from the road behind them. "I know you said the device was wiped clean, but does that prevent it from being tracked?"

"They can track it." He quickly powered the device off. He hesitated, hating to toss the phone Cass had paid for, but the possibility of her being hurt trumped concerns over money. He opened his window and tossed his brand-new phone out, wincing as it shattered on the ground. "If so, that's not a problem now."

There was a long moment of silence. "Okay, then," Steele finally said. "That takes care of one problem. However, it occurs to me that if these guys know you personally, they'll know where you work."

"Do you think the safe house is available?" Cassidy asked. "We could sure use it."

"That's not going to help. I need computer access," he quickly interjected. "I would rather work at the precinct."

"I'd rather you be safe," Cass shot back. "We can get one of our laptops to use at the safe house. It has internet access."

He was about to press the issue, but she had a good point about the safety factor. The precinct wasn't foolproof the way a safe house might be. "Okay, I'll go to the safe house as long as you stay with me."

"Do you remember the safe house?" She turned in her seat to look at him. "I don't think you've ever been there."

A vague impression of a brick house in a residential neighborhood flashed in his mind. A memory? How could he know? "I'm not sure."

"Call Rhy, see if the safe house is even available," Steele suggested. "It's often in use, especially for families."

The photograph of his mother and her husband flashed in his mind. Somehow Gabe had sensed he was not a part of their family. The picture on Steele's phone had been like seeing a stranger. Someone he knew from a distance, but not on a personal level.

Yet he must have communicated with Travis, otherwise how had his half brother's phone ended up smashed and broken at the same location where he'd been assaulted?

He glanced over his shoulder again, but there was no sign of the black SUV. If they had been tracking his phone, then they should be fine.

But he wasn't taking anything for granted. Not after he'd been used as target practice on three separate occasions.

Interesting that they'd let him live in the first place.

Maybe they had thought he was dead and had been in a rush to get away from the scene of the crime. Or they had figured he'd be in a coma or something. Having amnesia had certainly worked to their advantage.

No matter the reason he'd made it this far, it was obvious that these guys were trying to make up for their mistake of allowing him to survive.

He pressed his fingertips into his temples. Remember! He needed to remember!

"Rhy? Hey, a black SUV found us on the interstate and fired several shots. Steele's SUV is drivable," she quickly added, "but we think they may have tracked the replacement phone we picked up for Gabe. That's gone now, too, but we're wondering about using the safe house. We don't want to bring danger to the precinct."

Noticing Steele's concerned gaze in the rearview mirror, he dropped his hands and listened to Cassidy's side of the conversation.

"Yeah, I understand. We'll find another place to stay." She shot him a resigned look. "Keep us on the list, though. Thanks."

"Sounds like the safe house isn't an option," Gabe said flatly. "What's the next option?"

She shrugged, glancing at Steele. "What do you think? The American Lodge? Or some place we've never used before?"

"The American Lodge should work," Steele said thoughtfully. "I don't think these guys know about the tactical team, or they wouldn't take random shots on the interstate. They may not realize the resources we have at our disposal."

The American Lodge sounded very familiar. "Have I been there?"

"No," Cassidy assured him. "You booked it for us and send backup there as needed, but you have not stayed there."

"And we know the owner, Gary Campbell," Steele added. "He's supportive of the team and will give us rooms for cash."

"He also installed security cameras, which may come in handy," Cassidy said. "Let's head there now. We'll get Flynn or Jina to meet us there with a laptop."

"And a clean vehicle," Steele said with a scowl. "They may have gotten the license plate on this one."

Hearing the two of them discuss the best way to keep him safe made him wish he could do more. To contribute in some small way.

"Maybe you should ask one of them to bring me a gun."

Both Steele and Cassidy gaped at him. "What?" Steele echoed in shock. "That's crazy. You don't shoot guns."

"Do you know for sure I've never fired one?" he asked. "I mean, you guys are armed. Maybe I should be too."

"Look, Gabe, I know you asked for a gun earlier today. And I'm not necessarily opposed to giving you one. But as Steele said, as far as I know, you've never fired one, and that could be a problem. A gun isn't going to help you if you're not familiar with it."

"Cassidy is right. You could hurt one of us by mistake," Steele said. "We'll keep you safe."

"I hate feeling helpless," he said. Hurting one of them was the last thing he wanted. "I need to do my part in this."

"You will," Cassidy said, "by cracking the computer code on that USB drive you hid in the freezer. That could be the key to blowing this open."

"Okay, I'll do my best." He still felt as if he were more of a hindrance in this endeavor. Especially since Travis was still missing. "But once this is over, I want you to teach me how to shoot."

Cass and Steele exchanged a quick look. "Sure, Gabe," she finally said. "I'll take you to the firing range if you're still interested in learning how to shoot once your memory returns."

The way she said it seemed to indicate the Gabe she knew would never want to fire a gun. Was that true? He didn't know.

But he made a silent promise to follow through with learning how to shoot. Because he never wanted to be this helpless when it came to being in danger ever again.

"There's the American Lodge," Cassidy said, changing the subject. She gestured to the west side of the road. "The vacancy sign is lit, so that's good for us. I'm glad there are rooms available."

"Probably because it's the middle of the week," Steele said. "I know Gary is booked up on the weekends, especially this close to the holiday."

The two-story white building emanated a sense of familiarity, but Gabe had to assume it was only because he'd seen pictures. Maybe from their website? As Steele parked in front of the lobby, he knew he'd never been inside.

"Wait here, I'll take care of the room," Cassidy said.

"Use my cash." He thrust a wad of bills toward her. "Please. I want to contribute."

She hesitated, then took the cash. "Thanks. Be back soon."

Gabe watched her disappear inside. "I hate this," he said. "I hate knowing you and Cass are risking your lives for me."

"Gabe, you're an integral part of our team." Steele met his eyes in the rearview. "Of course, we're going to protect you. We protect strangers every single day. But when someone attacks our family, it's even more important than ever to seek justice."

He sighed and nodded. "I know that. It's just . . ."

"You care for Cassidy. A lot," Steele said. "Your feelings are no secret, Gabe. We've all noticed."

He felt himself flush. "Really? So Cass knows too?"

"I'm not sure about that," Steele said with a shrug. "She cares about you as a friend for sure. I don't know that she's figured out how much you want to ask her out."

"I—ask her out?" He was shocked at what Steele was saying. "There's no way she would go out with me."

"Gabe, you'll never know unless you ask her," Steele said with a grin. "Her last boyfriend was a real dud, couldn't handle her career. We're all rooting for you, hoping you'll take the next step. But for now, you may want to wait until your memory returns."

Her last boyfriend was a dud? And they were rooting for him? He couldn't believe how much Steele seemed to know about his feelings. More than he did, obviously. Before he could say anything more, though, he saw Cassidy pushing out of the lobby door.

She held up two room keys with a triumphant look on her face. She opened the passenger door, allowing a cold blast of air in. "Got 'em. Rooms 11 and 12 on the first floor."

"Okay. I'll park around the corner as usual," Steele said, driving past the lobby and making a loop toward the rooms Cassidy had obtained for them. "Glad he had the connecting rooms available."

"I asked Gary to keep an eye on the security cameras too," she said. "He said the place was only about half full, so doing that for us shouldn't be a problem."

"Gary's a frustrated cop at heart," Steele said with a

grin. "He loves helping us, as long as we don't damage his rooms."

"Hey, we always pay for the damage," Cassidy said. "And he's appreciative of that."

Gabe frowned. "You make it sound like we damage his motel rooms on a regular basis."

Cassidy grimaced. "Yeah, we kinda do. Although it's been a few months now since we've had any issues here."

"Oh yay," he muttered. "Score one for the good guys."

Obviously, he knew cops faced danger on a regular basis. But that didn't mean he liked the idea of Cassidy putting her life on the line for him. Or for anyone.

Was that part of the reason he hadn't asked her out?

There was no way to know what had held him back until his memory returned. Deep down, he feared that he had asked her out, but she'd turned him down.

And if that was the case, he needed to do a better job of keeping his feelings to himself.

CASSIDY SET their new disposable phones on the table and watched as Gabe examined the setup of their connecting rooms. She had sensed some trepidation on his part in staying here, but he seemed better now that they were settled in.

"How soon can I get that computer?" Gabe asked. "And I just realized we left our overnight cases in Rhy's car."

"I'll call Jina," Steele said, pulling out his phone. "We need a replacement vehicle, too, so this may take some time."

"Have her bring the computer first, then work on the vehicle," Gabe said, clearly impatient to get started.

Steele shot her a look, as if asking what's up with Gabe, so she stepped forward and rested a hand on his shoulder. "It's okay, Gabe. We'll have the rest of the day to work on the computer code. The replacement vehicle is important too. No sense in making Jina and whoever is available to help her make two trips."

Gabe sighed. "Okay. Sorry. I guess I'm still on edge from the shooting."

She understood his concern. Being targeted by gunfire was very much outside Gabe's comfort zone. She nodded at Steele. "Have Jina bring at least two computers, and our suitcases if she can."

He nodded, then crossed into the next room to make the necessary arrangements.

"You also mentioned calling your mother," she said to Gabe. "Let's get the phones up and running. Better to use one of them for that call. And maybe you'll learn something that will help you crack the code."

"Yeah, okay." Gabe reached for the phones and began unwrapping them. "Seems I've done this before."

"We all have," she assured him. "It's standard protocol when needing to stay off-grid. Just like getting a replacement vehicle. We know how to cover our tracks."

Steele came back into the room. "Jina and Flynn will be here in twenty minutes or so. Rhy has already arranged for a rental based on the gunfire incident, so it won't take them too long to get here."

"I forgot to ask you to call Rhy for Gabe's mother's number," Cassidy said.

"Hang on." A minute later, Steele was jotting down the number on a notepad. "Thanks Rhy. We'll stay in touch."

Gabe stared down at the number for a moment. She wondered if he was having second thoughts about contacting her, but then he dialed the number and listened. He frowned, glancing at her. "Leave a message?" he asked in a whisper.

"Why not?" she asked.

"Hi, uh, this is Gabe. I'm working on tracking Travis down but need to talk to you. So, uh, call me at this number." He rattled off the new phone number. Then without saying anything more, he disconnected.

"I'm sure she'll call back," she said reassuringly. "You reached out from a strange number, which most people assume is spam. I'm sure that once she realizes it's you, she'll get in touch."

"You're right." Gabe set the phone aside and then rose to his feet. "It's so hard to stand around doing nothing when Travis is in danger."

They didn't know for sure Travis was a victim, but she held her tongue. The smashed phone did lean that way. Yet she still believed Travis had been the one to lure Gabe out to the isolated location in the first place. Maybe Travis was asked to do that by someone else, but she felt certain Travis had made the call. Gabe was too smart to follow orders issued by a stranger.

Rhy was planning to retrieve Travis's phone records, which may provide more clarity. If the device hadn't been wiped clean the way Gabe's had been.

The code on the USB drive was the key. But even then, there was no guarantee that would help them find Travis.

"Hey, do you know a guy by the name of Marcus Toller?" Steele asked, glancing up from his phone. "He's in several photographs with Travis on social media."

"Doesn't sound familiar," Gabe said. "I'd like to see the pictures."

Steele handed over his phone. Gabe stared at the image

for a long moment. She leaned forward to see for herself. The guy was a stranger to her. But she understood why the guy had caught Steele's attention.

He wasn't a teenager, like Travis or his high school friends. For one thing, he dressed nicer and was clearly in his mid-thirties.

Roughly Gabe's age, if she had to guess.

"I don't recognize him." Gabe reluctantly handed the phone back. "When we get the computers, we can do a deeper dive on him, though. He doesn't look as if he has a criminal record, but it's worth checking out."

"Yeah." Steele went back to scrolling on his phone. "Travis has several friends his age, but this guy seems off. And the only photos of them are together, without any of Travis's other friends, so I don't think he's a high school coach or counselor."

"I agree. He stands out as someone my half brother wouldn't normally hang around with," Gabe said thoughtfully. "But it could be that he's a boss or a coworker. I have no idea where Travis works."

"If he works," Cassidy felt compelled to point out. "I'm getting the impression money isn't an issue, and if so, there would be little motivation for Travis to get a job."

Gabe frowned as if that thought hadn't occurred to him. "If he's not working, then how did he get involved in this?"

A rhetorical question, as no one had an answer.

They sat in silence for a few minutes. Gabe fidgeted in his chair, glancing constantly out the window.

Finally, Steele's phone rang. "It's Jina," he said, before answering it. "Yep, I see you."

Jina arrived at the motel first, after dropping Flynn at the rental agency to pick up the new ride. Steele let her in.

"Hey, Gabe." She set two computers on the table and

gave him a quick hug. "Heard you got bonked on the head and lost a few marbles."

Gabe reluctantly smiled. "Sounds about right." He reached for the top computer. "Thanks for bringing these."

"Yeah, it sounded urgent." Jina exchanged a concerned glance with Cass. "Several attempts of being shot at is not good. And I have no idea what you sent to my email, Gabe. It looked like something from NASA."

"I'm not sure what it's related to yet either." Gabe opened the first computer, pushing the other to the side, then quickly logged in. For the first time since they'd been at the precinct earlier, he looked comfortable with the task before him. "But I plan to find out."

"Let's let him get to work." Cass gestured for Steele and Jina to follow her into the adjoining room. Out of Gabe's earshot, she said, "I'm worried his half brother isn't an innocent victim in this. Finding Travis's phone at the spot where Gabe was assaulted makes me think Travis lured Gabe there for some reason."

"I'm with you on that," Steele said. "The phone was damaged on purpose, as if a heel had stomped on it several times."

"Could be Travis was forced to cooperate," Jina said. Cassidy knew the team's sharpshooter had softened a bit since she'd been a key suspect in a cold-case murder investigation. Jina could still toss most guys to the mat in record time, but she wasn't as quick to pass judgment as she had been. "And the bad guys smashed his phone to make a point of why he should continue to cooperate."

"It's possible," Cass agreed. "But either way, we need to do our best to work this case by focusing on Travis. That's why I asked for two computers. I know we would usually ask Gabe to help with this, but he's the only one who can figure out what he'd put on that USB drive, so it's up to us to pick up the slack."

"We can do our best," Steele said. "Maybe we start with that guy, Marcus Toller. See what we can dig up on him."

Satisfied they were on the same page, she turned to head back to Gabe's room. Flynn arrived with her duffel and Gabe's suitcase. She left Jina, Steele, and Flynn to the task of moving the vehicles around. Steele's damaged car would need to be dropped off at a body shop.

"Be careful driving my SUV back to the precinct," Steele warned. "The shooter may have gotten the license plate number. If these guys are tech savvy, the way we believe, they may be able to run the plate, tracking it back to me and those of us on the team."

Jina and Flynn exchanged a long look. "I'll take it," Flynn offered.

Jina shrugged. "Okay, but I'll stick close to you as we head back, just in case." She paused, then added, "Unless you need us to stick around?"

"No, we're fine." She glanced at Steele who nodded.

"Yep, we can manage," he agreed. "If I have to leave for some reason, I'll call one of you back. Or another member of the team."

She knew Steele's wife, Harper, was pregnant with their second child, but she wasn't due until April. Lately, the team members and their spouses had been doing their best to populate the next generation. At times, it made her feel lonely.

After breaking up with Wade Morris, she'd lost interest in settling down. Yet even as the thought formed, she found herself glancing over her shoulder into the connecting room to find Gabe hunched over the laptop. He'd run his fingers through his hair, causing strands to stick out at various angles. He looked different without his glasses, and the way he sat close to the screen made her think the contacts weren't working as well as he'd hoped.

She hated the idea of someone trying to kill him.

"Let us know if you find anything," Jina said, turning toward the door. "Oh, and we left the rental along the side of the building."

"Thanks." Cass had anticipated that, as they preferred not leaving their vehicles out in the open.

After Flynn and Jina left, she looked at Steele. "What do you think about continuing your search on social media while I use the computer?"

"Okay." Steele gestured to the connecting door. "Let's get to work."

She snagged the second computer and dropped into the chair next to Gabe's. Keeping the computer on her lap, she logged in and did a quick criminal background search on Marcus Toller.

He was clean. Or at least hadn't been caught. She did a broader search, hoping to find his name mentioned in some articles or other news outlets.

Still nothing.

The lack of progress made her cranky, and she was tempted to toss the computer out the window.

How did Gabe do this for hours on end? She couldn't stand it.

As if hearing her thoughts, Gabe leaned back and dug his palms into his eye sockets. "My head is killing me," he muttered.

"Take a break," she said. "We need you."

He lowered his hands and offered a rueful smile. "Thanks, but I'm still not being much help. I should remember this code," he said, gesturing to the computer.

"But all I can say with any degree of certainty is that it's an operating system of some sort. But to what program? And why is it so important?"

"You'll get there." She put a hand on his knee. "If anyone can crack it, you can."

"I want to believe that." He covered her hand with his, and she was suddenly aware that Steele had retreated to the other room. Maybe to sit at the table there, rather than taking over one of the beds. "I don't want to fail you, Cass."

"You could never do that." She smiled gently. "Suffering from amnesia isn't your fault. All we ask is that you do your best."

He held her gaze for a long moment. She set her computer aside and leaned over to hug him.

"You're going to figure this out, Gabe," she whispered in his ear. "I believe in you."

He wrapped his arms around her and held her tight. For a long moment, neither of them moved. She didn't want to let him go.

But then his new disposable phone rang. They jumped apart, as if the sound had been a gunshot rather than a shrill ring.

"Must be my mother," Gabe said, reaching for the phone.

She ran her fingers through her hair, doing her best to calm her racing heart. In that moment, she was forced to admit her feelings for Gabe had morphed from one friendship to something more.

And she was at a loss as to what to do about it.

CHAPTER EIGHT

Mentally bracing himself, Gabe answered the phone. "Hello?"

"Where's my son?" His mother's voice was a loud shriek, and he had to pull the phone from his ear. "What did you do to him?"

"I didn't do anything to Travis." He tried not to sound defensive and hoped he was telling the truth. The crushed phone flashed in his mind. Had he hurt Travis? No, he couldn't imagine doing such a thing.

"This is your fault! You have to find him!" His mother's voice rose in panic. "He's not answering his phone! He always has his phone. Always!"

"I have my entire tactical team working on finding Travis." He spoke in a firm tone, hoping to cut through her hysteria. "You can help by answering some questions. Can you do that, Mom? I need to know the last time you saw or spoke to Travis."

"You spoke to him last, not me!" she said in a voice that was slightly calmer. "You were the last one to see him alive."

That rocked him back on his heels. Although based on

finding his phone in the field where he'd woken up, it shouldn't have. "I saw him face-to-face or spoke to him?"

"How should I know?" The shrill panic was back. "He said he had to call you back as he walked out the door. You need to tell me what happened!"

He sincerely wished he could. "Mom, please try to remain calm. I need to know the last time you spoke to him. Yesterday? The day before? When did you notice him missing?"

"What are you not telling me?" she demanded. "Is he dead? Is that it? You don't want to tell me because he's dead?"

"No!" He winced, knowing that shouting back at her wouldn't help. "I have amnesia, Mom. I woke up outside with a huge lump on my head. I don't remember what happened, that's why I'm asking you these questions."

"Amnesia?" Her voice was a sneer. "Seriously? You really expect me to believe that?"

He raised his gaze to the ceiling, far too aware of the sympathetic expression in Cassidy's gaze. "You can believe what you want. I have no reason to lie to you. I am desperately trying to find Travis. If you refuse to help, then I'll figure out another way to get the answers I need to start tracking him down."

The silence stretched so long he'd wondered if she'd ended the call. Then the sound of sobs filled his ears. She was crying.

He told himself not to feel hurt at the way she cried for Travis, despite leaving him without a backward glance. "Mom, don't cry. It's going to work out."

"We had a fight," she said between sobs. "I didn't know he was in contact with you, and it made me angry."

"I'm sorry you argued with Travis," he said. "When was that? Yesterday?"

"Yesterday right after school." She sniffled loudly. "He took off in his new car, and I haven't seen him since."

"Tell me about his new car." He latched onto the news with both hands. "I need the make, model, license plate number."

"I gave all that to the other cop." He heard the sound of rustling paper. "Okay, I found it. Travis has a five-year-old Corvette convertible, metallic blue with a black top, and the license plate is DWE 7754."

He scribbled the information on the notepad. "Okay, that's great, Mom. I'm sure we'll be able to find that car. Just to be clear, the last time you saw Travis was at three thirty yesterday afternoon?"

"Yes." Another sniff. "He didn't answer my calls or text messages asking if he would be home for dinner."

"Does he usually answer you?" Gabe asked.

"No." The sobbing started up again. He had to wait for his mother to regain control. After a moment, she continued, "Travis can be stubborn, like any other typical teenager. He often ignores me. When I realized he didn't come home last night, I blew up his phone again, begging him to answer me. But he didn't! And he's never done this, Gabe. He's never stayed out all night without telling us."

"Okay, I understand." He did his best to soothe her fears, despite the sick feeling in his gut. He hadn't realized he may have been the last one to speak to Travis before his disappearance. "Maybe he lost his phone. Did the officer you spoke to issue a BOLO for the Vette?"

"How should I know?" She was getting angry again. "You did this, Gabe. I just know you're responsible for Travis disappearing. I need you to fix it!"

"I'll do my best," he said.

"That's not good enough! I want you to promise you'll bring Travis home. Promise me!"

"Mom, I will do everything humanly possible to find Travis. I won't make promises I can't keep. Thanks for calling me back." With that, he pushed the end button and tossed the new phone on the table.

Thankfully, his mother didn't call him back to continue ripping into him. He already felt more battered and bruised after that call than he had waking up in the snow last night.

"That was awful," Cassidy said in a low tone. "I'm so sorry she treated you so terribly."

"She's distraught." He raked his fingers through his hair. "I guess I can't blame her for being worried about her son."

"She has two sons, Gabe. Two!" Cassidy's blue eyes sparked with anger. "And she has no right to treat you like garbage."

He shrugged. "I can't change her attitude. All I can do is focus my efforts on finding Travis. And it sounds like I was the last one to talk to him."

She reached out to take his hand. "I heard most of the conversation but not all of it. Did she overhear you talking to Travis?"

He thought back through the painful conversation. "No, she said he was planning to return my call. They argued over us being in touch, then she saw him on the phone as he headed out to his car." He frowned. "He may have called me. Or left a message."

"If that was at three thirty, he would have had to leave a message because you were at the precinct until five," Cassidy said.

"Okay, that helps." The timeline of Travis's last movements was starting to take shape. "Travis left home at three thirty in the afternoon. Maybe he went to a friend's house because we hadn't connected yet. At some point, we must have talked and met up on the deserted road near the Wildflower Motel."

"Maybe he drove all the way to your house," Cassidy suggested, "and that's why your car was in the garage."

"It's possible, but I don't understand why Travis would hit me on the head and leave me outside in the cold. And where is he now?"

"Let's touch base with Rhy. Maybe he has more information regarding the BOLO for the Corvette." She pulled out her new phone. "A sweet ride like that shouldn't be too difficult to find."

He nodded, still feeling as if he'd been trampled by a herd of wild horses. He struggled to remember if Travis had been at his house, but he couldn't summon a single memory.

Hard to blame his mother for not believing him.

Dejected, he closed his eyes. *Please, Lord Jesus, help me remember!*

"Okay, thanks, Rhy," Cassidy said. "I'll let Gabe know."

He opened his eyes, wondering what he'd missed.

Her expression softened, and she took his hand again. "Sorry, Gabe, but there's been no sign of the Corvette. Based on finding Travis's phone earlier today, they've now broadened the search to include all of metropolitan Milwaukee, Madison, and every city in between. As far as Travis's phone records, Rhy is still waiting on them. Cameron is hoping to get them within the hour."

"That's good." He tried but couldn't summon a smile. "I really hope Travis is okay. That if he's involved, he's physically fine."

"We'll pray for him." She tightened her grip on his hand and bowed her head. "Dear Lord Jesus, keep Travis safe in

Your loving arms. Guide us as we search for the truth. Amen."

"Amen." He didn't release Cass's hand as he looked deep into her beautiful blue eyes. "Thank you. For everything."

"We're in this together," she assured him. Then she surprised him by leaning forward to brush a light kiss on his cheek. "We'll find him, Gabe."

He shouldn't have been so moved by her kiss, not when his half brother was missing. But he was. Oddly, between the prayer and her caress, he felt stronger. Letting her go wasn't easy, but he straightened and turned back to the computer. "This code has to be important, but darned if I can figure out how."

"I wish I could help, but the only code I know is the one to get into my condo." She gestured to the screen. "You mentioned this was likely code to an operating system. I assume it's clean? By that I mean not infected by a virus?"

He frowned, considering her question. The virus that had been unleashed on the precinct system could be related to this mystery code. "I don't know. Maybe."

He decided to start at the beginning, looking at it with fresh eyes. With an effort, he pushed the contentious conversation with his mother out of his mind.

Finding Travis was the only thing that mattered.

WATCHING as Gabe went back to work on the laptop, it took all Cassidy's willpower not to kiss him again. She felt terrible for what he'd suffered at the hands of his mother. Not just today, but the way she'd walked away and traded up for a new life. One she clearly had no intention of sharing with Gabe.

God didn't teach His children to hate, but for those moments she'd listened to Gabe's mother shriek one accusation after another at him, she'd seethed with hate. And anger. And the acute desire to reach through the phone connection to punch the woman in the mouth.

Whoever said violence doesn't solve anything never met Shelia McCord.

She blew out a soundless sigh and turned back to her own computer. Her search on Marcus Toller hadn't revealed much, but now she couldn't help but wonder if the guy was some sort of mentor to Travis.

With a mother like Shelia, she couldn't blame the kid for searching for guidance elsewhere. And where was his father in all of this? What was his name? Paul?

Too busy defending criminals to be of any help?

On a whim, she typed the name Paul McCord into the search engine. The top hit featured his name and professional photograph as a partner in the law firm of Wendel, Baker, and McCord Law.

She clicked on the link to scroll through the website. McCord appeared to be the youngest of the group and likely the more recently added as a partner. They touted their amazing success without giving specific details as to which criminals they'd successfully represented to an acquittal. The headline "Wrongly Accused" caught her eye.

Without identifying anyone by name, there was a brief summary explaining how a man who'd been wrongly accused of murder had been set free thanks to the hard work and dedication of Wendel, Baker, and McCord. She tried to remember the story from the news but couldn't.

There was no date listed, so the trial could have been a few years ago.

Whatever. It probably wasn't associated with Travis's disappearance. She clicked out of the website and went back to Marcus Toller. She pulled up his DMV records to check his address. Of course, he lived in Madison, which was well over an hour away.

Call Roscoe to ask Cameron to do the interview? Or drive out there themselves? As much as she wanted to speak to the guy personally, it was a risk to head out with Gabe. Especially since they didn't know anything about this guy.

She reached for her phone.

"Yeah?" Roscoe's hesitant tone reminded her that she was calling from a strange number.

"Hey, it's Cass. I'm with Gabe and Steele. We're working the case of Travis McCord. Have you spoken to your cousin Cameron?"

"Hey, Cass, I heard about what happened to Gabe. Yes, I've spoken to Cam. Between you and me, Gabe's mother is a piece of work."

"You have no idea," she said wryly. "The reason I'm calling is that we found a guy by the name of Marcus Toller on Travis's social media. He looks too old to be a student, and I can't find anything about him through normal channels. I'd like Cameron to track him down and ask him about Travis."

"I'm on it," Roscoe said without hesitation. "I'll let you know what Cam has to say after chatting with him."

"Thanks." She ended the call and set the phone aside.

"Cass?" Steele stepped across the threshold of their connecting rooms, his expression grim. "Joe sent out an alert asking the team to respond to an active shooter at the Milwaukee Mall."

"Go," she said, knowing that a crime in progress had priority over their current situation. She tossed him the keys Flynn had left behind. "Take the rental."

Steele didn't hesitate. A moment later, he was gone.

"Is that something you'd normally respond to?" Gabe asked.

"Yes." She shrugged. "But I'm sure the team can handle it without me."

He frowned, holding her gaze. "I get the sense I'm both a part of the team yet separate from the team."

"You're the hub of our team," she said. "In a situation like this, you would be at the helm, digging into any information regarding the incident. And once we had a name of the shooter, you'd feed us even more intel. We all depend on you, so don't minimize your role. It's important."

He nodded. "That makes sense. And I can see why you wouldn't want me to have a gun."

Why was he was so focused on having a weapon? "Gabe, it's nothing personal. If I knew for sure you could hit what you're aiming at, I'd get one for you."

"Wish I could remember that too. Among other things." He turned back to the computer. "I haven't found anything that resembles a virus. But there are a few anomalies that are bothering me."

"In what way?" She had no idea what he meant. "Like maybe there was a virus, but someone removed it? Similar to the way you got our precinct system back up and running?"

"No." He shook his head and sighed. "I'm not sure what it is. There are a few spots that appear to have been altered. Without knowing what this operating system runs, I can't say how or why the changes were made. Just that they are not congruent with the original code."

More gobbledygook. But it was sweet that he assumed she understood. "I wish I could help, but all I can say is to trust your instincts."

He blinked and rubbed his eyes. "My headache is getting worse."

"Too much screen time." She frowned. "Take a break. Get some rest."

"Not an option." He glanced at the clock. "It's quarter past two in the afternoon. Travis has been missing for nearly twenty-four hours. You know as well as I do that we need to strike before the trail goes cold."

"We don't know for sure when he went missing," she said. "Could be that it wasn't until later that he ran into trouble. Besides, we're not letting the trail go cold. Every cop is on the lookout for Travis's car, and Cameron is going to interview Marcus Toller. The investigation is ongoing."

He didn't look at all reassured, likely because he was still riding the guilt trip his mother threw in his face. Cass hoped she never had to meet the woman because she'd likely add fuel to the fire by setting her straight on her warped priorities. Like brutally reminding her that she has two sons that she should care about. Not one. Two! And Gabe deserved as much care and consideration as Travis.

But imagining a confrontation with the woman wasn't helpful. Especially since God would want her to practice forgiveness. And she would.

Eventually.

She was searching Travis's social media when her cell phone buzzed. She frowned because the only people who had that number were at the scene of the active shooter.

"Hello?"

"Is this Cassidy Sommer? Officer Sommer?" a male voice asked.

"Yes, may I ask who you are?"

The guy chuckled. "Sorry, this is Cam. I got your number from Roscoe. Apparently, he's a bit tied up at the moment."

"Yes, they're out on a call." She felt a little guilty about staying behind. "Did you find Marcus Toller?"

"I did. He's a math teacher at the high school where Travis attends classes," Cameron said. "Apparently, Travis is some kind of math whiz, and Toller has been helping him to get into a college that specializes in computer science, specifically gaming. From what I gather, Travis's parents don't approve. According to Toller, Travis was told to become a lawyer, or he could pay for his college on his own dime."

The more she heard about the McCords as parents the less she liked them. "I guess that explains the social media posts. Does Toller have any idea what happened to Travis? Did the teenager confide in him?"

"No. He claims the last time he saw Travis was when he left school at the end of the day yesterday. He wasn't aware of anything specific that Travis was concerned about. Other than not being supported by his parents."

Gabe glanced over, clearly listening. She gave him a nod, indicating the news was good. Or at least not bad. "I'm glad Marcus Toller has been supportive of Travis."

"According to him," Cameron said. "But my gut says he's telling the truth."

She heard a beeping on the other end of the line but ignored it. "We should still check out his whereabouts for yesterday afternoon and evening," she said. "Just to cover all bases."

"I did that already. His alibi checks out. He stayed late at school to tutor kids who are not so good in math. From there, he went home to his wife to have dinner. If he's involved with Travis's disappearance, he's doing an admirable job of hiding it."

"Okay, thanks, Cam." The beeping had stopped, and she wished she had a smart phone to know who had called. Probably Rhy with an update on the mall shooting. "I'll fill Gabe in on the latest. He'll be glad to know that Toller was helping his half brother get into college."

"Later," Cameron said, and ended the call.

Before Gabe could ask her to repeat the parts of the conversation he'd missed, the phone in the adjoining room began to ring. At first, she was confused as to who could possibly be calling.

Then she knew. Gary!

She bolted through the connecting door, suddenly desperate to get to the phone. She grabbed the receiver just as gunfire rang out.

"Cassidy! There's a shooter across from room eleven!" Gary shouted.

"Call 911!" She dropped the phone and pulled her weapon. In a low crouch, she ran back toward Gabe's room.

He was on the floor beneath the table, cradling the laptop computer to his chest. It was smart to use it as a shield.

She ducked as more gunfire rang out. "The bathroom," she said, gesturing to it. "Get into the tub and keep your head down."

"What about you?" Gabe asked, his brown eyes full of concern.

No question they were in a tough spot. Steele had taken the rental, leaving them without a quick way to escape. "I'll hold them off until the cops arrive."

"Then I'm staying with you," Gabe said.

She wanted to yell at him, but that would be a waste of time. "Follow me, then. We're heading to the other room."

She duck-walked through the connecting doorway with Gabe following. So far, the shots had peppered the room Gabe had been sitting in. Their only advantage was that the shooter probably didn't know about the connecting rooms.

It wasn't much, but she edged toward the window, staying to the side as she scanned the wooded area across the parking lot. She knew that area well, as several other shooters had positioned themselves there to pepper the motel with bullets.

They really needed to stop using Gary's motel as a safe house.

She caught a glimpse of movement. She held her breath, waiting to see more. There! A dark shadow near a tree. She lifted her service weapon and pressed the tip up against the glass window. It wasn't optimal to fire through glass, but she would if necessary.

There was a lull in the shooting, giving her the impression the gunman was trying to figure out if he'd eliminated his target.

"Come out where I can see you," she whispered. "Come on, show your face."

Another flash of movement followed by another volley of gunfire. This time, she was forced to duck to the side as their window was struck.

Apparently, this guy was hedging his bets. What if he decided to take out more windows? She couldn't sit there while innocent people were hurt.

Or worse.

She popped her head up and fired toward the shadow. Then she dropped back down to where Gabe was huddling beside her.

Where was the Brookland PD?

Cold air streamed in through the broken windows. Then she heard sirens.

She took another quick peek over the windowsill, but this time she didn't see any movement near the trees. The silence stretched from ten seconds to twenty, then thirty seconds.

The shooter was getting away!

She jumped up and reached for the door, just as Gabe snagged her hand. "Wait, where are you going?"

"We need to find him!" She shook off his grip, then paused. All Gabe had for protection was the laptop. She couldn't leave him alone and vulnerable. She abruptly dropped back down to her haunches. "Never mind. The Brookland PD is already on their way. They'll fan out to search for this guy."

Gabe looked torn between telling her to go and asking her to stay. She couldn't blame him; it was a toss-up for her too.

"We'll find him," she said reassuringly. "Hopefully, Gary caught his image on the cameras."

Three Brookland PD squads squealed into the parking lot, and several cops dressed in tactical gear jumped out and hunkered down behind the squads.

"He took off!" Gary shouted. "I was watching the camera when he took off!"

Instantly, the cops jumped up and spread out to search. But Cass instinctively knew it was too late.

The shooter was long gone.

CHAPTER NINE

This being shot at was really starting to piss him off. And he hated knowing that Cassidy was under fire like this on a regular basis.

Not that he didn't admire her skill and bravery, because he did.

"Stay here for a few minutes." She stood and pulled the door open.

"I'm coming with you." He still had the laptop and wasn't willing to leave it behind. His headache had gotten much worse the longer he'd worked. He was about to take a break when the bullets had started flying.

Cass shot him an annoyed glance as she strode toward the Brookland PD officers who'd responded to the 911 call. "I'm MPD tactical police officer Cassidy Sommer, and this is Gabe Melrose, our tech expert. We need to fan out and search for the shooter."

Gabe didn't recognize any of the cops and decided that wasn't a memory issue, but more that he'd never been in Brookland under these circumstances before. He was impressed that the officers dressed in tactical gear did as

Cassidy ordered, one pair spreading out to search the tree line and another pair going around to the back of the motel.

"Cassidy? Are you and Gabe okay?" Gabe turned toward the male voice coming from the lobby doorway. He hadn't met the man, but he assumed he was the owner, Gary Campbell.

And from the looks of their two motel rooms, they'd once again caused significant damage to the place. Both windows of the rooms were broken, and the drywall inside was pockmarked with slugs.

He felt bad they'd brought danger to his doorstep.

"Yes, we're fine," Cassidy called. "Do you have video for us?"

"I do, but the perp is wearing a ski mask and was dressed in black." Gary came out to survey the damage. "Wow. Looks bad."

"I'm sorry, but you know we'll pay for the repairs." Cass patted Gary's arm. "And we'll put a rush on that so it's ready by the holiday."

"That would help," Gary said with a sigh. "I am booked solid starting two weeks before Christmas."

"I'm really sorry," she said again. "We took precautions. I have no idea how we were found."

Gabe thought back to the call he'd received from his mother. On his side, he'd used a new disposable phone. But his mother obviously hadn't. Was it possible someone had infiltrated her electronics? Deeply enough to track her phone call to his location?

It was possible, and that made him feel even worse. "I think it's my fault."

"No, it's not," Cassidy swiftly said. "You're a victim in this, Gabe."

Her support was touching, but she wasn't following.

"No, I mean, I think it's possible someone traced the call my mother made to me from her phone to this location."

"How?" Cassidy asked with a frown.

"I'm not sure, but the technology is there and accessible for those who know how to exploit it. Everyone has their homes wired up these days. They use their wireless internet to log onto their TVs, their phones, and computers. They'll use a central device to turn items on and off, choose songs, and that kind of thing." He shrugged. "I suspect that somehow these guys are tapped into my mother's home network."

He didn't add that Travis likely could have done that without breaking a sweat.

"Okay, now you're really freaking me out," Cassidy said. "If these guys can do that and shoot guns, we're at a distinct disadvantage."

"I told you I should have a weapon too." Even as he said the words, though, he knew he wouldn't find it easy to shoot at a person. Unless, of course, that person was aiming at Cassidy. He swallowed hard, and added, "But that's not going to help us find Travis. Or understand why these guys have targeted me."

"Clear!"

"Clear!"

One by one the officers cleared the area. Cassidy watched grimly as the four of them returned to the parking lot. It was both a relief and a frustration. He shared Cassidy's desire to grab and arrest this guy. But he was just as glad the danger was over.

For now.

"Thanks for responding so quickly," Cassidy said. "We'll need the crime scene techs to get here to retrieve any slugs and shell casings."

"There are several casings on the ground between the trees," one of the officers said. "He didn't bother to recover his brass."

"I'm not surprised. He was moving too fast to worry about that." Cassidy scowled. "I doubt we'll find prints, but it's worth a shot."

Two off the officers went over to gather the casings.

Another SUV pulled up. Gabe half expected Rhy, but it was a pair of detectives who emerged from the vehicle. He could see their gold badges clipped to their belts.

"Must be the new guys," Cassidy murmured. He wasn't sure what she meant but couldn't ask as she stepped forward. "MPD Tactical Officer Sommer."

"Detectives Olsen and Rippon," the taller of the two men said. "What happened?"

"Our tech expert Gabe Melrose has been assaulted and targeted by gunfire several times over the past twenty-four hours," Cassidy said. "We came here to stay off the radar. Unfortunately, the gunman found us."

Detective Rippon turned to face him. "Why are you being targeted?"

"I'm not sure. I'm still trying to figure it out." He didn't want to explain his memory loss. "I think it has to do with some sort of programming code. I wish I could tell you more, but I haven't figured it out yet."

The detectives exchanged an incredulous look. "Seriously? That's all you have?"

"Yes, or we wouldn't be staying in a motel trying to avoid being shot at." Cassidy waved her hand at the broken windows. "As you can see, that didn't work out so well for us."

"Why do I feel like you're holding back?" Detective Olsen asked. "We might be new detectives in Brookland, but we're well aware of how Rhy Finnegan tends to swoop in and steal cases that belong to us."

"Hey, does anyone want to see the video?" Gary asked, interrupting what Gabe sensed was a bitter argument.

"Yes, I do." Gabe turned to see Cass nod in agreement. "And I'd like a copy of it as well."

"We need that too," Detective Rippon said.

"Figured you would, I'll make copies for both departments." Gary turned and led the way inside. Gabe and Cassidy crowded on one side of Gary, while the two detectives took the other.

The video quality wasn't bad, and Gabe wondered if he'd had any input into what Gary had purchased. His stomach tightened when he saw the dark figure dressed in black moving quietly through the trees, gun in hand.

"I told you he was wearing a ski mask," Gary said apologetically, as if he should have been able to do more with his cameras. "But you can see that he takes several shots, ducks behind the tree when Cassidy returns fire, fires another series of shots, then disappears from view."

"Can you zoom in to see his clothing better?" Detective Rippon asked.

"Sure." Gary zoomed in. "Just looks like basic black jeans, black leather jacket, black gloves, and black ski mask."

"Not helpful," Cassidy said with a sigh.

"Nope." Detective Olsen glared at Cassidy. "Are you sure you don't know who this guy is or why he's after your tech expert?"

"If I did, I'd find him and arrest him." Cassidy's blue eyes flashed with anger. "I want him and his cohorts caught as much as you do."

"What makes you think this guy has accomplices?" Rippon asked suspiciously.

"Just a hunch." Cassidy held up her hands. "I don't know what we're dealing with, other than he keeps finding us."

"Where would you like me to send the video?" Gary asked, interrupting again. "I have Gabe's contact information, but I need yours." He gestured toward the two detectives.

Gabe stepped back, giving Cassidy room to move out of the small office. She reached for her phone.

"Wait." He put a hand on her arm. "Not sure we should be making calls from here."

"We're not staying, and we need a ride." She glanced over her shoulder at the two detectives. "I doubt they're willing to drop us off at the car rental agency."

He grimaced. "Is it always territorial like that?"

"We used to be on better terms with the Brookland PD because Rhy lives a few blocks from here. But after last month, things have been tense."

He wanted to ask what happened last month, but Cassidy's phone rang. "It's Rhy," she said, before answering. "Hey, Rhy, we're fine, but the shooter got away."

Gabe scanned the area. listening as she filled their boss in on the recent events.

"Okay, thanks, Rhy." She lowered the phone. "Roscoe is on his way to pick us up. The scene at the mall has been secured, the shooter is dead on scene, and the five victims are being rushed to Trinity Medical Center. No officers were hurt."

He was glad to hear the crisis was over, but it wasn't good that it had taken place at all. Shootings in general had gotten out of control. Not just those individuals with a personal vendetta, but those seeking notoriety or lashing out in anger.

It made the shootings targeting him pale in comparison.

He glanced down at the computer. Was that why he'd chosen to fight crime from behind a desk using a computer as his only weapon?

Man, he really wished he could remember.

"Come on, let's get back inside to wait for Roscoe." Cassidy tugged at his arm. "It's cold out here."

The Brookland detectives didn't say anything as they walked by, but Rippon was on the phone, his expression betraying his anger. "Yes, sir," he said. "I understand."

Cassidy waited until the lobby door shut behind the detectives. "I'm sure Rhy has been in touch with their captain." A smile tugged at the corner of her mouth. "Our boss has a way of getting what he wants."

From his interactions with Rhy Finnegan, that wasn't a surprise. He was about to ask again about the incident last month when Cass's phone buzzed.

"Hey, Roscoe." She listened for a moment, then said, "Yep. We're here in the lobby. See you in ten." She tucked her phone away. "We'll be out of here soon."

"Good. What about our suitcases?"

"They'll have to stay here until the crime scene has been cleared." She shrugged. "Not important now."

"Yeah, okay." He couldn't deny he was glad to put this recent shooting behind him. In that moment, it struck him how close they'd come to dying today. And not for the first time.

He set the computer on the lobby sofa, then turned to face Cass. He reached out to draw her close. Without allowing himself to talk himself out of it, he brushed a kiss over her mouth, giving her plenty of time to back away or even to slap him.

She didn't.

Instead, she wrapped her arms around his neck and pulled him closer, deepening their kiss. His heart soared as he held her close.

If he'd ever kissed her before, he felt certain this time was different. Better. Far, far better than anything he might have imagined.

And he wished he never had to let her go.

BEING HELD and kissed by Gabe was amazing. So much so that Cassidy wondered why they hadn't done this before.

"Did you get the—oh, sorry." Gary sounded cheerfully apologetic. When Cassidy broke off their kiss, she could see the motel owner grinning at them. "Just wanted to be sure you got the video."

"I, uh, Gabe?" Flustered, she glanced over as Gabe picked up the laptop he'd tossed onto the sofa.

"Checking now," he said, looking adorable with the tips of his ears burning red from acute embarrassment. As if he'd been caught stealing a cookie.

It helped to know the impact of their unexpected embrace was not one-sided. Although she couldn't help but wonder if Gabe would have kissed her if he had his memory back.

Somehow, she didn't think so.

"Um, yeah. I have it," Gabe said a moment later. "And it opens without difficulty. Thanks."

"You're welcome." Gary was still grinning like a fool.

She caught a glimpse of a black SUV pulling up to the lobby. "We need to go. Roscoe's here." She nodded at Gary. "I'll talk to Rhy about fast-tracking the repairs."

"I appreciate that." Gary's smile faded as the seriousness of the situation returned to the forefront of their minds. "And stay safe. Both of you."

"That's the plan," she said, heading toward the door.

The cold wind slapped them hard as they headed outside. Funny, she hadn't noticed it as much when they were outside watching the search for the shooter.

With a shiver, she slid into the front next to Roscoe. Gabe took the back.

"Hey, heard you're having memory issues." Roscoe turned to glance at Gabe. "I'm sorry to hear that. And that you've been targeted by gunfire."

"Thanks." Gabe's smile didn't reach his eyes. "I hate knowing Gary's place was damaged because of me."

"The shooter is responsible, not us," Cass said quickly. "None of this is your fault."

"I don't know," Gabe said in a low voice as he stared blindly out the window. "I feel like it is. That I somehow started this mess but can't remember how or why."

She exchanged a long look with Roscoe, not knowing how to reassure him. Even if Gabe did somehow set these events in motion, she was convinced there was a good reason.

Too bad they were no closer to figuring out what exactly that entailed.

"Do you want another rental car?" Roscoe asked, drawing her attention from her troubled thoughts. "Everyone is planning to meet back at the precinct to debrief."

Did they need another rental car if Steele was bringing the one Flynn had already gotten for them? Probably not. "Heading back to the precinct is a good idea for safety reasons." She frowned. "I really wish the safe house was available."

"Yeah, I hear you." Roscoe shrugged. "We'll figure something out."

She didn't point out that so far their efforts had been in vain. Then again, she wasn't sure what they could have done differently. It had never occurred to her that Gabe's mother's phone could be tracked through her home network to the American Lodge. She twisted in her seat to look at Gabe. "I thought the reason we use passwords on our home security networks is to prevent people from hacking into them?"

"It is," Gabe said, "but nothing is foolproof."

"But if that's the case, how do we prevent hacking?" She scowled. "You're making it sound as if anyone can get access into our private homes."

"Not easy," he said, "but not impossible either. Keep in mind, Travis is missing."

Now she understood. "You think Travis could have given the bad guys the password to the network."

"Yes. Or one of his techy friends already had it." Gabe's expression turned grave. "I'm worried Travis is working against us on this. That he somehow got in over his head with some really bad actors."

She wasn't sure how to respond. She wanted to believe they'd find Travis alive and well and not doing anything illegal. "Either way, we'll find him."

Gabe frowned. "I hope so."

They arrived at the precinct at quarter past four in the afternoon. Past shift change, but she knew from experience Rhy would work as late as needed.

Roscoe parked next to the rental. The three of them climbed out and headed inside. The rest of the team was already assembled in the conference room.

"We're not sure what the shooters motives were," Steele

was saying as they entered. "I suspect the feds will be all over this."

Rhy nodded. "I spoke to my brother Brady; he's got their tech expert Ian Dunlap digging into the shooter's background. He'll let me know when they find something."

"Why do I get the feeling that's a task I should be doing?" Gabe asked as they sat in the three empty seats.

There was a pause before Rhy said, "I probably would have asked for your help, but these shootings are being investigated as domestic terrorism, which means the feds would be involved no matter what."

Cassidy could tell that Gabe was upset at not being able to help, so she redirected the conversation. "Gabe was explaining to me that his mother's home internet security could have been breached by the bad guys, and that's how we were tracked to the American Lodge."

Rhy's eyebrows shot up. "Really? How is that even possible?"

She was glad she wasn't the only clueless one. She waved at Gabe, indicating he should explain.

"The easy answer is that Travis or one of his friends gave out the password. But the truth is any network can be hacked. And Travis's home may have been targeted on purpose in a cyberattack."

"Great, another thing to worry about," Brock muttered. "As if we don't have enough violence on the street, now we have to worry about cyberattacks."

"Cyberattacks have always been a problem," Joe said. "But until now they hadn't been used to target law enforcement activities."

There was another moment of silence as that sank in.

"We need to figure out how to keep Gabe safe," Cass

finally said. "Especially since he needs to keep working on the computer code we found in his freezer."

"Those are words that have never been in the same sentence before now," Raelyn said in a low voice to Jina.

Grayson grinned and shook his head. "Nope."

"Whatever." Cass waved a hand. "What's the plan? We can rent a place, but how long will we be able to use the internet before it's hacked?"

"They'd have to find us there first," Gabe said. He used both hands to rub his temples as if to ease his headache. "And I hate to admit it, but I may need some rest. The screen time is making my headache worse. I was having trouble seeing the code when the shooter found us at the motel."

She hadn't realized how difficult working on the code had been for him. Was that the reason his memory hadn't returned? "Of course, you should rest. You suffered a horrible injury, and we need your mind to heal."

"Yeah, well, I also need to find Travis," Gabe said. "But there's not much I can do when the screen goes blurry."

"We need to take you to Trinity Medical Center," Grayson said.

"I'll support that, too, but when Sami had amnesia, doctor's orders were basically to rest, which meant no screen time at all—television, computer, or phone," Rhy said. "We haven't been following that treatment plan since this happened."

"No hospital, but I will have to concede on the rest issue." Gabe grimaced and pressed harder on his temples. "My stomach is churning again, just like it was after I woke up from being attacked."

Now she was concerned. She jumped up and tugged on his arm. "Come on, let's get you into the equipment room."

"Go," Rhy said. "That's an order."

Gabe must have felt bad enough that he didn't argue. But he paused in the doorway to glance back at the team. "Please wake me up if you get news, good or bad, on Travis."

"We will," Cass assured him. "I promise."

Rhy nodded in agreement. "Of course."

She walked with Gabe to the equipment room where they had two cots. "Get some sleep." She didn't kiss him again, the way she wanted to.

He stretched out with a sigh and closed his eyes. "Thanks," he whispered.

She closed the door and quickly returned to the conference room. Everyone turned to look at her when she walked in. "What?" she asked, confused by the attention. "What did I miss?"

"Nothing," Joe said with a wry grin. "We're discussing how to arrange for a rental. We're thinking of asking Rhy's brother-in-law Bax Scala to help with that."

"Good idea to use the DA's office to secure a rental property rather than using the City Central Hotel," she said. Rhy's sister Kyleigh Finnegan now Scala married Bax last year. Bax and Maddy Sinclair, formerly Callahan, both worked as ADAs for the city of Milwaukee. The Callahans, the Finnegans, and their tactical team all worked together to fight crime.

But this was the first time Cass felt as if they were out of their depth. The computer aspect of this case had them at a disadvantage.

Especially with Gabe's amnesia hampering their progress.

"Yeah, Bax specifically asked us to stop going to the

City Central," Joe said with a sigh. "Apparently, bullet holes are not reassuring for the witnesses who stay there."

Rhy grimaced. "That's an exaggeration; the bullet holes were fixed. And it's not our fault that gunmen tracked us down there. But I agreed to stay away for a while."

"Don't forget to fix Gary's motel rooms," Cassidy said. "I promised him that we would."

With a nod, Rhy said, "I made those calls while I was waiting for everyone to get here. The glass guy will be there first thing in the morning."

"To get back to the cyber security problem, can we ask the FBI's tech guy for help?" Jina asked. "I'm not sure what he can do for us, but without Gabe, it feels like we're shooting in the dark without ammo."

"Good idea," Rhy said, rising to his feet. "I'll talk to Brady about that. I'm sure Ian won't mind taking a look at Gabe's mystery code."

After Rhy left, the rest of them sat silent for a moment. Then Cassidy said, "I'll stay here, but the rest of you should head home to your families." It was a stark reminder that she was the only nonmarried or engaged member of the group. And several of the guys had pregnant wives. Last she'd heard, Raelyn and her husband, Isaiah, were actively trying to conceive too. "I'll call if we come up with anything."

"I don't have to rush home," Jina said.

"Me either," Raelyn added.

"Go, please." She waved them off. "There's nothing any of you can do."

And that included her.

Her teammates filed out, each giving her a quick one-armed hug to show their support. They'd barely left the precinct when Rhy poked his head out of his office. "Cass? They found the Corvette."

She sucked in a harsh breath as she hurried over. "Where?"

"Abandoned in a park-and-ride lot about five miles from where you and Gabe found Travis's phone." Rhy looked grim. "They also found a smear of blood on the rear panel."

"The trunk?" She wasn't a car expert, would a body even fit in the trunk of a Vette? "Is Travis . . ."

"The trunk is empty," Rhy said quickly. "The local crime scene techs are heading out to take a sample of the blood for testing."

Blood on Travis's car. She swallowed hard, glancing toward the equipment room where Gabe was sleeping.

The news was concerning. Was the blood an indication Travis was hurt?

Or worse, dead?

CHAPTER TEN

A split second after he'd closed his eyes and relaxed into the blessed darkness, Cassidy shook him awake. "Gabe?"

He groaned, cracking one eye open. She was blurry, and he threw out his hand to reach for his glasses. Then he remembered he was wearing contacts. The blurriness was because of his head injury.

"What?" He forced himself to wake up. With both eyes open, he could see her more clearly. Sort of. The room was still relatively dark with a little ambient light coming through the open door. He focused on her face, noting her concerned features. "What's wrong?"

"They found Travis's blue Corvette. No sign of Travis or any obvious damage to the vehicle. It was located about five miles from the spot where you were assaulted." She held his gaze for a long moment. "There was a little blood on the quarter panel. Not a lot, but the crime scene techs are there and will send it for testing."

"Blood? Travis's blood?"

"We don't know. Try not to think the worst." She sat

beside him on the cot. "To be honest, I have been wondering if the blood is yours. Maybe from the wound on the back of your head."

His blood? The image of Travis's blue car flashed in his mind. A memory? He wasn't sure. "If my head hit the car, there would be a dent."

The corner of her mouth twitched in a smile. "True, you do have a hard head. But from what Rhy has been told, there's no dent. Could be you wiped it with your hand or something equally innocuous."

He hoped the blood was his, not Travis's. He wished he could have gotten more sleep, the pounding in his head wasn't that much better, but there was work to do. He pushed himself to his feet, then swayed.

"Hold on, where are you going?" Cassidy jumped to her feet and stepped in front of him to grip his arms. "You need to rest. I only woke you because I promised."

"Can't." It was all he could do not to collapse back down to the cot. He steeled his resolve. "There's no time. We need to find Travis."

"How? You don't have anything to go on."

He hated to admit she was right. Especially now that they'd found Travis's car. That had been the one connection they had to his half brother.

Now they had nothing.

"The code," he muttered mostly to himself. "The answer to where Travis is and who has him must be in the code."

"A code you're in no condition to look at right now," Cass said firmly. "Seriously, Gabe, I'm begging you to get more rest. We need your help to run down the computer stuff."

"What time is it?" He didn't have a watch, and there was no clock in the equipment room.

"It's almost six," she said. "You've been sleeping about an hour."

An hour? Not a handful of minutes? He winced, realizing he was in worse shape than he'd thought. He blinked again, struggling to focus. "An hour is more than I realized. It should be enough of a break that I can get back to work."

"No." Her steely tone took him aback. "I mean it, Gabe. I almost didn't wake you up because I knew you'd try to get right back on the computer. Are you hungry?"

Hungry? Normally, he would be, but the nausea that swirled in his gut indicated otherwise. "Not really."

She threw up her hands. "See? That's my point! You're not well enough to work."

"I'll eat." He managed to stay upright. "Please, Cass. We'll grab something to eat, and then I'll work for a bit." When she opened her mouth to argue, he added, "If the screen gets blurry again, I'll stop."

"Promise?" She looked deep into his eyes, and even though the only light was coming in through the open door, he could see she was truly concerned.

"Yes, I promise." He forced a smile. "I appreciate you keeping your vow to wake me with news. I'll keep my promise as well."

"Fine." She released his arms. "But I'm only giving in because I think you should eat something. The fact that you're not doing any snacking is just as concerning as hearing you admit your vision has been getting blurry."

Having seen his drawer of snacks, he couldn't argue the point. After watching him for a moment, she gave an exasperated sigh, then turned away. "Rhy ordered pizza. I hope that's okay."

"Sure." Gabe followed her out of the room, wincing when the bright lights hit his eyes. Maybe he should consider working while wearing sunglasses. Then he knew if he did that, Cass and Rhy would make him stop. Remembering she said the time was six o'clock, he frowned. "Rhy should be home with his wife and daughter."

"I told him that," Cassidy said, glancing at him over her shoulder. "He's worried about you, Gabe. We all are."

"I'm fine." Cassidy's concern was heartwarming from a personal perspective, but he wasn't an invalid. He didn't want Rhy or the other members of the team to pity him. A memory caught him off guard. Two months ago, Zeke had gotten shot in the shoulder while protecting his fiancée, Sienna, from harm. Zeke had gone through emergency surgery to repair the damage and was still getting physical therapy while being off work. That was something to be concerned about.

Not a bump on his hard head.

Yet there was no denying his concussion was hampering his ability to work.

When he followed Cass into the break room, he was relieved only half the overhead lights had been turned on. The throbbing in his head dimmed a little. He crossed to the staff fridge and pulled out a water bottle.

"You should be sleeping," Rhy said, entering the room carrying a large pizza box.

"Yeah, and you should be at home with your wife and daughter," he shot back, getting annoyed. He decided not to mention remembering Zeke as it wasn't helpful to the case.

Cassidy chuckled but quickly turned it into a cough when Rhy glared at her.

"Wow, it smells great." Gabe nodded at the pizza, surprised that it wasn't a lie. The tangy tomato sauce and cheese were an enticing combination. "Thanks for getting it."

"It's the least I can do," Rhy said.

"I'd like to say grace." Cassidy glanced at him as they took their seats around the small rectangular table. Rhy nodded and bowed his head. "Dear Lord Jesus, we ask You to bless this food, keep us safe in Your care, and guide us to the truth. Amen."

"Amen," he said, wondering why God answered some prayers but not others. He desperately needed his memory to return to save Travis. But so far, that particular prayer had gone unanswered.

"Amen," Rhy echoed. "And as Roscoe would say, dig in."

The three of them ate in silence for a few minutes. The pizza was loaded with the works, the way he liked it. When Rhy's phone rang, he startled badly.

"It's Ian," Rhy said as if noticing his reaction. "I asked him to help." Rhy answered the call. "Hey, Ian. I hope you have good news."

Gabe understood why Rhy had gone to the FBI for help, but he couldn't help feeling annoyed. The computer code was his problem. He should have been able to figure out what it was for as he'd obviously saved it for a reason.

Yet he also knew they needed all the help they could get to find Travis.

Rhy frowned, and his hopes for the latter plummeted. "Okay, Ian, I understand. Any help you can give us is appreciated. I'll be in touch tomorrow." He lowered the phone to the table. "Ian has no idea what the code is for, and he's been reassigned to work on the mass shooting case from the mall. Apparently, the kid who did the shooting had been digging around in the dark web. Ian has been asked to follow the kid's trail to find out more. The concern is that there's some sort of network of kids who are chatting on the dark web about shooting as many people as possible. If there is something along those lines, it's important to find it before anything else happens."

"That's understandable," Cassidy said. "A bummer for us but understandable."

"Yeah." Rhy looked at him. "I want you to rest up so you can get back to work. I'm not kidding, Gabe, we need you."

"I promise to work only as long as my vision remains clear," Gabe said. "Maybe just another hour or two at the most."

Rhy and Cassidy exchanged a look of concern, but his boss didn't argue. "I'll hold you to that," Rhy said. "If I catch you squinting at the screen, you're done for the night."

"I'll watch him like a hawk," Cassidy added. "You need to get home, Rhy."

They continued eating their pizza, and Gabe was surprised the meal gave him a burst of energy. Maybe he had been hungrier than he'd realized.

Yet the moment he sat back down at his computer screen, his headache intensified. Must be related to his concussion, but looking up the symptoms he was already experiencing seemed counterproductive. Since his vision was clear, he decided to start over at the very beginning of the code.

He took his time, trying to imagine what operating system the code belonged to. Had he copied it from somewhere? He didn't think he'd created it. Then again, maybe he had but couldn't remember.

A quarter of the way through his review, he realized there were levels to the code. Some of the lines repeated, but then went on in more depth. What did that mean? Was it possible Travis had gotten the code from the dark web, like the teenager who took a gun to the mall to shoot as many innocent victims as possible?

The dark web was a definite possibility, but as he continued to work, the numbers on the screen began to blur together. He sat back and pressed the heels of his hands against his eyes seeking relief.

"That's it. Time's up." Cass emerged from behind him, reaching over his shoulder to take control of the mouse and closed the program. "You promised."

He had, and the truth was that he couldn't wait to get back into the darkness of the equipment room. "Okay. But I feel bad making you stay here all night."

"There are two cots in the equipment room," Cassidy said with a shrug. "We'll be safe there."

He nodded and pushed away from the desk. It was weird to share the equipment room with Cassidy, yet the moment he stretched out on the cot and closed his eyes, he sighed in relief.

And fell instantly asleep.

WHEN CASSIDY CAUGHT herself staring at Gabe through the darkness, she sat up and tiptoed out of the room.

It was too early to sleep anyway, and the cot wasn't exactly as comfortable as a full mattress. Keeping an eye on the clock, she headed back over to Gabe's desk. There were a handful of cops working, but most were out on the street.

Exactly where she would have preferred to be.

A couple of the officers and detectives eyed her curiously. She was self-conscious about being out of uniform.

The hours ticked by slowly. At a quarter to midnight, she stood, intending to head into the equipment room, when the phone on Gabe's desk rang.

She automatically reached for it. "Milwaukee Police Department District Seven."

"Gabe? Are you there?" The whisper was so quiet she could barely hear. She couldn't even say for sure if the caller was male or female.

She plugged her ear with one finger to drown out the ambient noise. "This is Officer Sommer. I can have Gabe come to the phone, but I need to know who's calling."

There was such a long pause she feared the caller had hung up. But then she heard, "Please get Gabe."

Was this Travis? She decided not to push the issue of the caller identifying him or herself. "Okay, stay on the line." She carefully set the phone down and bolted to the equipment room.

"Gabe. Wake up!" She shook his shoulder. "I might have Travis on the phone. Hurry."

"Travis?" Gabe blinked in shock, but then quickly sat up. "Are you sure?"

"No, I'm not sure, but the call came through on your line, and the person is asking for you."

Without saying anything more, Gabe strode from the room. She quickly followed, her heart pounding with antici-pation. Maybe Travis was being held against his will but managed to escape long enough to make a call?

"Hello? This is Gabe, who is this?" With the receiver pressed to his ear, he glanced at her, shaking his head. "Hello? Is anyone there?"

His hopeful expression crumpled. Gabe replaced the handset and turned to look at her. "We need to trace that call."

"You're the one who usually does that," she said. "Did you hear anything? Voices? Breathing? Anything at all?"

He shook his head. "Nothing but dead air. Makes me think he disconnected before I was able to get here."

"I assume Travis knows your work number?"

He shrugged. "I have no idea if he's called me here before or not. If that was Travis, then yeah, he must have memorized it." His brow furrowed. "I hope that's not someone's idea of a prank."

"I don't think so, the voice was a low whisper. It was hard to hear and made me think the caller was trying to hide the fact that he was using a phone." She gestured to the computer. "Is there some sort of report you can run to find the number?"

"I'm looking." Gabe turned and logged into the system. His hair was mussed, but his brown eyes were clear. Maybe the couple hours of sleep had helped.

She watched over his shoulder as he accessed a part of the system that she'd never seen before. Then he clicked into the search bar of the program and typed in the phone number to his desk line.

A series of phone numbers bloomed on the screen. He quickly scrolled to the bottom for the most recent call. Grabbing a pen and paper, he jotted the number down. "Does this look familiar?"

"Not to me," she said. "I guess it doesn't look familiar to you either."

"No, but we can run this through another program to see if the phone belongs to someone who has registered it," Gabe said. He shot her a quick glance, adding, "The alternative is that it's a disposable cell."

Cass held her breath as Gabe worked. When he groaned, she asked, "What?"

"I was afraid of this. A disposable cell." He raked his hand through his hair, then said, "I can track where it was purchased, but we won't be able to go see the store video until morning."

A solid eight hours from now, maybe longer. Some stores didn't open until nine or ten. "Do your best, Gabe. Once you have the location, we'll be on their doorstep the minute they unlock the doors."

He did so, using another program she'd never seen or heard before in her life. She had always depended on Gabe to support her and the other members of their time while they were in the field, but until now, she hadn't realized the extent of his knowledge. The way he toggled from one computer system to the next was mind-boggling.

"Um, Cass?" He shot her a quick glance. "I found the store location, and you're not going to believe this."

"What?" She rested a hand on his shoulder as she leaned forward to see the screen. "What does that data mean?"

"It's the store locator." He brought up another program on an adjacent monitor. "That's the store that sold the phone where the call came in. Look familiar?"

Her eyes widened. "That's the same store we used to buy our phones."

"Yep." He tapped the screen. "I had a feeling that I'd find it here because the number is very similar to ours. This phone was purchased before ours, based on the ID number. Although I guess someone could have reordered the stock by accident."

The same store. "It's eerie to think that our bad guys were at that store shortly before or after us."

"Yeah." He sighed. "I'm tempted to call the number back

to see if anyone answers. But what if Travis is in trouble? Maybe he got ahold of the phone long enough to make the call but had to put it back before anyone noticed he borrowed it?"

She tightened her grip on his shoulder. "I don't think you should call it. At least, not yet. But can you trace it?"

"Maybe." His eyes brightened at the possibility. "It should work as long as the phone is still on. But if not, I won't be able to see the signal bouncing off the towers."

"I have confidence in your ability, Gabe," she said with a smile. "You can do it."

He grinned, then turned back to his computer screens. She stepped back to avoid giving in to the temptation to kiss him again.

Why were her feelings changing like this? She and Gabe were friends, nothing more. For all she knew, Gabe wasn't interested in dating a cop either. Like Wade Morris, who'd decided the danger was too much for him.

She turned and paced, sending up a silent prayer for God to help them find Travis before it was too late.

Too late for what, she wasn't sure. Was the teenager in danger? Or had he gone along with the plan but now had changed his mind and wanted out?

She turned to grab a snack from Gabe's desk drawer. When she pulled on the handle to the right-hand drawer, she frowned when she saw her favorite candy inside. "You don't like KitKat bars," she said.

"I don't?" Gabe barely glanced at her. "I must have stuffed a few in there for you."

She stared at his profile, wondering when he'd done that, then grabbed the candy bar.

"I found it!" Gabe's voice rose with excitement. "It pinged off this cell tower here." He tapped the screen. "It's not perfect, the phone could be anywhere within a five-mile radius, but it's a place to start."

Munching the candy, she nodded in agreement. "Let's take a drive. Maybe we can narrow down a few likely places where Travis and others could be hiding out." She glanced at the time. "I don't want to drag Rhy, Joe, or the others out in the middle of the night without something more to go on."

"Agree." Gabe jumped to his feet and grabbed the closest laptop. He opened the computer and quickly logged into the same program that was still displayed on his screen. When he had it, he turned to her. "I'll bring this with me. If the phone dings off another tower, we'll know they're on the move."

"Sounds good." She finished the candy bar and tossed the wrapper into the garbage. "I want to grab some gear from the equipment room first, though."

He didn't complain, although she could sense his impatience. Not that he wanted to bypass safety procedures, but the ping of the disposable cell phone was the only tangible lead they had to Travis.

One he was desperate not to lose.

The vests she grabbed weren't specifically fitted for her or Gabe but would do in a pinch. She hoped they wouldn't need them. She carried them to the rental and threw them into the back.

Traffic was quiet this time of the night, so it didn't take long to reach the cell tower.

"Wait a minute, is that the Wildflower Motel?" Cassidy asked.

"Yes." Gabe divided his attention between the laptop and their surroundings. "The cell tower is fairly close to the location where we found Travis's phone."

And the spot where Gabe had been assaulted. She exited the interstate and turned left to head south. "I find it hard to believe they'd have grabbed rooms at the Wildflower Motel, but stranger things have happened."

"I don't think that's the spot either," Gabe said. He frowned as she drove past the area that crime scene techs had combed through earlier in the day. "I'm thinking more like a warehouse or a home that they may have rented. Someplace where Travis wouldn't have easy access to the phone." There was a pause, then he added, "If that was Travis on the line."

She wished she could reassure him, but the caller had barely said ten words and none of them loud enough to assume gender.

When they reached the end of that road without seeing anything, she turned to head west. "This area is more remote," she said by way of explanation. "East takes us closer to the civilization."

It took longer than she anticipated to drive up and down each street, searching for a likely hiding spot. Because of the late hour, most houses were dark, but as they came across addresses, Gabe made a note of them and tried to find them on home rental apps. The process was painstakingly slow. She was about to call an end to their efforts when she saw a restaurant and bar called the Homerun that had a for sale sign out front.

The parking lot was empty, and as it was going on the 2:00 a.m. bar time, she felt certain the building was empty. At least, supposed to be empty.

"What do you think?" she asked, as she drove past without stopping.

Gabe nodded slowly. "It's within range and an empty building that someone could be using on the sly."

"Risky, though, since it's possible the owner could stop by. Or the real estate agent could arrive with a potential buyer." She frowned, trying to imagine Travis being held inside. "Maybe we should make a note of the place and head back."

"Wait! Pull over!" His voice rose with excitement. "I think this could be it. Looks like it's been on the market for over forty-five days. Let's sneak up and look inside."

She hesitated, then did as he asked. It couldn't hurt to check the place out. Especially if it has been on the market for a long time. Clearly no one is champing at the bit to buy it. She turned in her seat as she killed the engine. "We put the vests on, and I'll take the lead. You stay behind me, okay?"

He frowned but nodded. He shut the laptop, tucked it under his seat, and slid out of the vehicle.

Putting the vests on didn't take long, she helped Gabe with his after donning hers. Cassidy drew her weapon and took the lead in crossing the field toward the supposedly vacant building. As they silently approached, she told herself if she saw anything remotely suspicious, she'd get Gabe out of there and call Rhy and the others for backup.

There was no visible light coming through any of the windows. She led Gabe all the way around the building first, examining the ground. She found several sets of footprints; they crossed over each other so she couldn't isolate one to estimate size. Could be from the real estate agent, anyone. Or kids checking the place out.

The back door was locked and likely led to the kitchen. There were no windows back here, so she crept around to the side of the building.

She sidled up to the closest window and peered in using her small flashlight to illuminate the area. The main seating area consisted of several tables and chairs that looked a tad beat up. At first, she didn't notice anything unusual.

Then she saw it. A small disposable phone sat in the center of one table. A replica of the one she'd purchased for her and Gabe.

And it had obviously been left behind on purpose in a heart-wrenching message.

CHAPTER ELEVEN

"Travis could be in the basement," Gabe whispered, his heart thudding painfully against his ribs. Seeing the cell phone in the center of the table had rattled him. Badly.

His half brother must have been here. Maybe still was.

"I'll call for backup," Cassidy whispered back.

"No time." He tightened his hand on her arm. "The phone provides reasonable suspicion and exigent circumstances."

"That's stretching the rule," she said with a frown. He released her arm, fully intending to break in through the back door himself, when she quickly added, "Okay, fine. I'll find a way to make it work. Just stay behind me."

He was grateful she'd agreed to enter the building. She turned and made her way around to what was likely the kitchen entrance. The door was locked, but Cassidy kicked at the doorjamb—once, then twice, then a third time. There was plenty of power behind her kicks, and he had a brief image of her working out in gym clothes when the damaged frame gave way. She pulled it open and peered inside. She took the lead because she was armed and had the flashlight.

He stayed behind her as ordered, glad he was tall enough to see over her head.

The interior was dark, and the heavy scent of grease hung in the air. The interior was warmer than the outside temperatures, but not by a lot. *Probably enough to keep the pipes from freezing,* he thought. As they made their way through the kitchen, there were obvious signs that someone had been there.

Recently.

Empty food packages were strewn about, and dirty dishes were stacked in the sink. No signs of bug infestation from what he could see, which was why he felt certain the items had been left in the past twenty-four hours. It wasn't a stretch to imagine the bad guys hanging out here with Travis, hopefully sharing their food with the teen.

Cassidy held her flashlight along the top of her weapon, sweeping the muzzle from side to side as they walked through the kitchen and into the main restaurant bar area.

He was impressed with her thoroughness as Cass made quick work of ensuring the main level was empty. The phone on the table mocked him, but he didn't reach for it. First, they needed to find Travis if he was still there. Cassidy checked both bathrooms, but they were empty. Glancing at him, she headed back into the kitchen toward the door on the far side of the room that likely led to the basement. Upon opening the door, he saw a steep staircase shrouded in darkness.

He almost called out to his brother, but Cassidy's stealthy movements gave him pause. What if someone was down there waiting for them? Maybe even holding Travis at gunpoint?

He silently descended the staircase behind her, doing his best to follow her lead, stepping where she did to minimize the noise. The beam of her flashlight played along the wall until it ended. The pizza churned in his stomach, even though the darkness was a balm for his headache.

By the time they reached the uneven concrete floor, it was clear no one was down there. He wasn't sure if he should be relieved or upset that Travis hadn't been left behind, bound and gagged. The good news was that they hadn't stumbled across his half brother's dead body.

Cassidy played her light over the floor and the walls. "No sign of a disturbance, no blood or bindings to indicate anyone was held down here." She glanced back at him. "Could be we're on the wrong track in assuming Travis was here."

He shook his head. "I'm sure he was. Let me examine the phone. If the number matches the one that called my office, we'll have our connection to Travis."

"We suspect the caller was Travis, but he never identified himself, so it could have been someone else," Cassidy said in an annoyingly reasonable tone as they headed back up to the kitchen. "A friend Travis trusted enough to provide the necessary information to make the call."

He understood she was being pragmatic, making judgments based on evidence, not his gut feelings. Sure, anything was possible, but the most likely scenario was that Travis had made the call.

Once they'd reached the kitchen, he strode straight to the main dining and bar area. He would have scooped up the phone without thought, but Cass stopped him.

"Don't touch it," she warned. "The phone is evidence that needs to be examined for fingerprints."

"I just need to see the number," he protested.

She pulled a small plastic bag out of her pocket and used it like a glove to pick up the phone. She gingerly turned the device so that he could just barely read the serial number on the back.

It took him a minute to visualize the phone number and serial number of the phone that had called his office. The actual phone number wasn't on the device, but the serial numbers were a match. "This is the phone used to call my office," he said with certainty. "The caller definitely was here when he reached out to me."

She nodded. "Which is why the phone was left on the table in plain sight. Whoever is involved wanted us to know that they discovered the distress call was made and that they've left the hideout to prevent us from finding them."

Hearing her state the obvious hit hard. It wasn't good that they'd taken off, leaving the phone behind. He didn't want to imagine the worst, but these guys hadn't balked at shooting at him and Cassidy. He knew they could take their anger and frustration out on Travis by physically beating him. Were they angry enough to kill him?

What if they found these guys too late to save his brother?

"Don't, Gabe," Cassidy said, reading his thoughts. "If they had killed Travis, I'm sure they'd have left him here. They didn't, which leads me to believe they're kept him alive for a reason. Because they need his skills, or they need him to draw you out. I suppose it's possible they're waiting to get to you before taking any further action. Hard to say for sure since we don't have a clue what this is about."

"No, we don't." And he desperately wished they did. "They must want the code that was tucked away in my freezer. I need to understand what it's for and soon. Before things spiral any further out of control."

She offered a reassuring smile, then stepped back to call the local police. He listened as she identified herself as an

MPD officer who needed assistance to investigate a poten-tial crime scene. As she explained what she needed, he glanced around the messy kitchen, knowing better than to touch anything, but searching for clues just the same.

"We'll get the crime scene techs out to search for prints," Cassidy said when she'd finished making the call. "I highly doubt these guys wore gloves the entire time. There's bound to be a partial print somewhere." She frowned. "Although connecting prints to the bad guys and not the previous bar owner's employees may add a layer of complexity."

"These wrappers look recent," he said, bending over to sniff at the grease that clung to the paper bag. "French fries and burgers likely." He didn't remember enough about Travis to identify his favorite foods and wished for the hundredth time that his memory would return. "We don't know how many people are involved, so it's hard to say if they spent a handful of hours here or had been using this as a hideout since yesterday."

Pursing her lips, Cassidy surveyed the area. "Yeah, I agree. We should focus our efforts on the empty wrappers, along with the dirty dishes in the sink. I highly doubt the previous owner and his or her employees would have left them behind."

"Probably not if they were hoping to sell." A wave of hope lifted his spirits. "How soon can we get those prints run through the system?"

"I'm sure Rhy will expedite the evidence processing," she assured him.

He nodded, then frowned when he saw the corner of a napkin peeking out from beneath an empty bag. "Cass, is there writing on this napkin?"

"Let me see." She drew on a pair of gloves and moved

the bag aside. "No writing, just a scribble as if someone was trying to make a pen work. Maybe the intent was to write a note, but there wasn't time."

"What about identifying the place where they bought the food?" he asked. The idea of Travis wanting to leave him a note but being unable to made him feel guilty for taking so long to get here. If they could have moved faster . . .

"There's a receipt in the bag, looks like it came from a place not far from here." She shrugged. "We can head over in the morning and ask if they remember anyone matching your brother's description being there recently." She shrugged. "Maybe something about your brother or the other guys was memorable."

"Maybe." He wasn't sure why any fast-food worker would remember a routine sale of food items.

"Hey, don't give up hope." Seeing his expression, she reached out to pat his arm. "Let's stay positive. This was their first mistake. They realized Travis or his friend made the call to you and bolted out of here. We have them on the run, which means they're likely to get sloppy again somewhere along the way."

He appreciated her attempt to keep him from spiraling into despair, but the fact remained that Travis was gone, and their only lead was the phone he'd used to call into the station was now a dead end.

Travis and the guys he was with could be anywhere. Driving one or more unknown vehicles.

They'd been so close to finding Travis, and now it seemed as if they were further behind than ever.

He closed his eyes and prayed.

Please, Lord Jesus, guide us to the truth. Help my mind

heal and grant me the strength and knowledge I need to find Travis! Amen.

CASSIDY DREW GABE outside when the local cops and crime scene techs arrived. She felt bad that they hadn't found Travis, but she was hopeful the crime scene techs would find fingerprints.

The hour was twenty minutes past three in the morning by the time she and Gabe were free to go. "I think we should head back to the precinct." She glanced at him. "There's time for you to get more sleep."

"I've been off screen for several hours now," Gabe said firmly. "I'd rather get back to work. I can't help but think Travis is in more danger now than ever. We can't afford to waste any more time."

"Rest isn't wasting time when you can't even see the screen clearly," she protested. "Come on, Gabe. You've been doing everything humanly possible to find Travis."

"Doesn't feel like it," he said with a sigh.

She knew his mother's guilt trip was weighing on him. And yes, if Gabe had his memory, they'd be much further along in understanding what in the world was going on. But they could only work with what they had.

Which wasn't much. A phone, some fast-food wrappers, and dirty dishes.

The local cops and crime scene techs had agreed to fast track the evidence when they learned a missing teenager was suspected to have been held there as an unwilling captive. She was glad she hadn't needed to wake Rhy to sway their decision.

She only hoped that these guys weren't smart enough to

force Travis to make the purchase, divvy up the food, and stack the dishes.

"There's something about that code that makes me think the answer is staring me right in the face," Gabe muttered. He tipped his head back and closed his eyes. "What am I missing?"

She had no answer. Concentrating on driving, she frowned when a pair of headlights flashed on behind her. Tightening her grip on the steering wheel, she increased her speed, putting more distance between them.

Within three seconds, the car behind her did the same.

Had the bad guys left someone behind to watch the restaurant? Fearful of a trap, she pushed the SUV faster. At the upcoming intersection, she abruptly turned left.

"What's going on?" Gabe asked, his eyes opening in alarm.

"We picked up a tail." She wished she'd considered the possibility of someone keeping an eye on the restaurant before now and quickly reviewed her options.

There were only two. Implement evasive maneuvers to lose the tail or head back to the restaurant where the officers were likely still hanging out.

Based on the lack of traffic and being in a more rural area, she settled on option two. Better to be safe than sorry.

With an abrupt move, she hit the brake and cranked the wheel. The tires squealed in protest as she sharply turned and drove out into the empty field to the west. The SUV bumped over the hard and uneven terrain, but she continued turning the wheel to make a circle around the car that had been following them.

Her maneuver must have caught the driver off guard because the car slowed without trying to follow. She hit the gas, sending their SUV surging forward. Less than a minute later, they were back on the road heading in the opposite direction, back toward the restaurant.

In the rearview mirror, she watched the car continue down the street away from them. "Alice, Henry, King, 4," she said. "Alice, Henry, King, 4."

"What?" Gabe looked at her in surprise.

"I only caught the first few letters and number on the license plate." She tried to remember what the vehicle had looked like. "I think it was a black SUV, like the one who tailed us before. But color can be deceiving in the darkness; it could have been gray, dark green, or dark blue. And I wasn't quick enough to get the make or model."

"A partial plate will narrow down the possibilities," Gabe said with excitement. "Especially if you know it's an SUV. I'm sure we can identify who the car belongs to. I'll run it through the system when we get back."

"Good. I hope we get a hit." Even as she said the words, a sliver of doubt moved in. Had she overreacted to the possible tail? If that guy behind them was one of the bad guys, he gave up the chase rather quickly. Was that because he knew they weren't far from having police backup? Maybe.

Yet if the driver of the SUV had been watching the restaurant for them to arrive, why not ambush them while they were inside? Unless the driver hadn't seen them right away, and by the time they'd been noticed, the local cops had shown up.

Thinking back, she estimated they hadn't been in the building for longer than fifteen minutes before the cops arrived. She had kicked the door in, though, so that should have attracted their attention. Unless they were too far away to have heard the noise?

She was driving herself crazy with theories. No point in

second-guessing her actions. It wasn't like they had a lot of other clues to follow up on. And running the partial plate wouldn't take that long. Well worth the effort to get a lead. She could go through the list of vehicles while Gabe went back to his mystery code.

She pulled up beside one of the squads at the restaurant, then lowered her driver's side window. "Hey, any chance you'd be willing to escort us back to the Seventh Precinct of Milwaukee? I just shook a tail off and don't want to run into another problem."

"Okay," the cop agreed, after a subtle glance at his watch. His partner shrugged, too, as if to say, *Why not?* "I'll let the other officers know we'll be off scene for a while."

"Thanks." Cass had pegged them for a couple of rookies who were often assigned to the graveyard shift. It was nice of them to offer to drive well outside their jurisdiction to shadow them back to Milwaukee.

She executed a three-point turn. The officer of the squad pulled out behind her. This time the trip to the precinct was uneventful. So much so that she felt a little guilty for taking the officers so far out of their way.

"Thanks," she said, waving them off. The driver acknowledged her with a return wave, before hitting the gas and heading back the way they'd come.

"At least they weren't territorial," Gabe said as she killed the engine. Reaching beneath the seat, he pulled out the laptop. "After our last encounter, I was expecting the worst."

"They were decent," she agreed. "Generally, cities that have smaller departments are less concerned about jurisdiction than larger ones. They tend to accept their limitations and are more often grateful for additional assistance."

"That's the way it should always be," Gabe said as they headed to the side entrance of the precinct.

She shrugged. "Keep in mind, we wouldn't be so anxious to hand off a case to another precinct either. Especially one that involved one of our team members. Which is mostly when we end up operating outside of the city."

He grimaced and nodded. "I see your point."

At his desk, they shrugged out of their coats and removed their protective gear. She was glad they hadn't been in a position to need it but decided not to put everything back in the equipment room. She wanted the vests handy if they had to head back out again.

"I'll start with the partial plate," Gabe said as he logged into the computer. "I'll run a list."

"Send it to me," she suggested. "I can comb through that while you focus on cracking that code."

"Okay." His fingers danced along the keyboard, making quick work of the task. A moment later, he'd sent the file to her email.

"Thanks." She pulled the file up on her phone, grabbed the closest chair, and settled down to review it.

She took each vehicle one at a time, instantly bypassing any pickup truck, minivan, or light-colored vehicle. For sure those were not the vehicles she'd passed. Once she'd eliminated those possibilities, four names were left to investigate in more detail.

Grabbing the laptop Gabe had brought in, she started checking the DMV registrations for each of the four vehicles. The first belonged to an elderly man, the second to a middle-aged woman. Since their children could have used the vehicle without their knowledge, she couldn't cross them off completely.

But the third car was a black SUV belonging to a

twenty-eight-year-old by the name of Miles Wayland. Without being judgmental, she took note of Miles's long, stringy dirty-blond hair, a scowl on his features, and hard eyes.

Miles moved up the suspect list, but that didn't stop her from investigating the fourth vehicle too. That was a blue Honda SUV that was registered to a sixteen-year-old girl by the name of Patrice Curtis. Based on the DL photo, the girl looked as if she could be a high school cheerleader. Pretty face despite the extensive makeup, hair stylishly curled, and a broad smile. Maybe Cass was being sexist, but she struggled to imagine this girl shooting at them.

Yet her age being so close to Travis's nagged at her. What if this girl was involved? She could have loaned her car to someone. Or she could be the driver while someone else fired the weapon.

Maybe she needed to keep Patrice on the list. Miles first, then Patrice.

"What did you find?" Gabe asked, sensing her dilemma.

"Do any of these four names sound familiar?" She recited them one by one. When he shook his head, she sighed. "Miles looks sketchy, but that doesn't mean he's guilty. And Patrice is close to Travis's age. Could be she lured him in somehow."

"Yes, but you can't ignore the other two," Gabe said. "We need to eliminate them completely before dropping them. They could have criminal backgrounds or family members with a criminal history."

"I understand. But I still want to start with the most likely prospect." She entered Miles Wayland into the system first. After a few minutes, she decided that if they were going to keep working until sunrise, they needed coffee.

She stood and headed to the break room. She watched Gabe work from the doorway as the coffee dripped. He'd run his fingers through his hair again, making it stand out on end. For his sake, she hoped Travis wasn't hurt. And that he wasn't involved in the criminal side of this thing.

Whatever it was.

She filled two cups with coffee, doctored them the way she and Gabe liked it, and carried them out to the desk. Gabe offered an absent smile as he took the cup and sipped.

Rather than ask if he'd learned anything new, she turned her attention to her task. Miles Wayland did not have a criminal record, which was disappointing.

Neither did any of the other three vehicle registrants.

Since that didn't work, she went back to the elderly man, Oliver Haydon. She ran a report of his known associates, which were mostly family members.

None of them had criminal records either.

She went through the same process with the middle-aged woman, Debra Flacko. She had even more known associates, but the only name that popped with a criminal record was a teenager who'd been caught selling marijuana.

Doubtful that selling marijuana would lead to firing shots at them, so she went back to Miles and Patrice.

Time to dig into their social media sites. She started with Patrice, mostly because in her experience girls were more likely to post online than boys.

Patrice was no exception. She had been right about the girl being a cheerleader; there were several posts featuring her alongside her fellow cheerleaders. She checked to see if Travis was a friend of hers, but he wasn't.

There was a post about her new (albeit used) car that was a gift from her parents on her sixteenth birthday.

Again, she couldn't see this girl being involved. Which left her first choice of a suspect, Miles Wayland.

Miles didn't have much of a social media presence. She found him on one site, but it was clear he hadn't posted anything in over two years. The other sites had even less activity.

There was one post that caught her eye. "Gabe, what is Dorian?"

"Huh?" Gabe turned to look at her. "Dorian?"

"Yes. This Miles guy has a post that says something about being on Dorian. That was two years ago, and he hasn't posted anything since."

"Dorian is a social media site for gamers." Gabe's eyes widened, and he abruptly turned to stare at his screen. "That's it. Gamers. This software is for a game!"

She wanted to be happy about the breakthrough, but she didn't understand it. "Like what kind of game?"

"A computer game. That's what those levels were about." He smacked his hand on the desk. "I should have known right away that this was related to a computer game."

"Okay, but why would a computer game cause you to be in danger?" A horrible thought hit. "You didn't steal proprietary software, did you?"

"Steal it? No." Gabe frowned, then said, "Although I did copy it here on the USB drive for a reason."

His comment was like a pin popping a balloon. Just knowing this was somehow related to a game wasn't enough.

They needed to understand why anyone involved with a computer game would want to kill Gabe.

Before they could strike out at him again.

CHAPTER TWELVE

Gabe's thoughts whirled as he stared at the computer screen. He was so close to uncovering the truth. The final piece of the puzzle hung just out of reach. He stared at the screen so long the numbers and letters blurred. He closed his eyes for a moment, trying to clear his head.

"Gabe? Can you tell me more about this gaming software?" Cassidy asked.

"Not really." He opened his eyes and focused on her anxious expression. "Let's take a moment to review the facts. Travis is a gamer and so is this guy, Miles Wayland. Maybe they met on the Dorian site. I can log in and check any communication that's public. But if they were in touch on the site in private, that will be more difficult to find."

"Okay, that's good to know." She smiled encouragingly. "Do you think Travis sent you this code?"

"I believe so, although I'm not sure why. But if he did, Travis may have done that via the same site." He turned and quickly brought up the Dorian gaming site. He typed in the password that came to his fingertips, but it didn't work.

He frowned, sitting back in his chair. He needed to

think this through. The last thing he wanted to do was to lock himself out by trying every password under the sun. He could go the password recovery route, but he didn't have a phone to verify his account.

Then he remembered his phone password, using Cassidy's name. He leaned forward, took a deep breath, and typed in *Cassha$myheart*.

It worked! He sent up a silent prayer of thanks as he quickly checked his messages.

"Is that the Dorian site?" Cass leaned over his shoulder to see the screen. "I've never heard of a specific site just for gamers."

"It's quite the community." He scrolled through the list to find the most recent messages from Travis. His heart thumped against his chest as he saw there were several messages from his half brother. "This is the message in which Travis sent the code." He scanned the cryptic message accompanying the document. "Seems he has concerns about the security of the game."

"Security?" Cass sounded skeptical. "That doesn't seem like something important enough to kill for."

"Maybe the computer software company thinks Travis was stealing their technology." He wished the messages were clearer, but it was obvious that Travis hadn't wanted to put the details in writing. Which was probably smart, as someone figured out what Travis was up to anyway.

"Okay, check this Miles Wayland guy, see if you can find his posts," Cass urged. "Maybe that will give us more information to go on."

He found Miles Wayland, but there were few public posts and nothing specific about gaming security. Although Wayland did mention the game Sorcerer's Sword. A chill snaked down his spine as he brought up the code he'd stored on the USB drive.

Was this the security system for Sorcerer's Sword, the hottest computer game to hit the stores in over a year? And if so, why had Travis been concerned? Was there malware embedded in the code?

Yet that didn't make sense. Gaming software was set up to get gamers hooked on making their way from one level to the next. The goal was to have the consumer invest time and energy playing it. Some companies even sold advertising that provided additional income to the company. If there was a hint of computers going down after playing the game, the entire gaming community would get the word out, and everyone would stop buying the product.

He was missing something, but what? Gabe rubbed his eyes, battling weariness. The sleep he'd gotten didn't seem nearly enough now that the rest of the day was looming before them.

"I found Miles Wayland's address," Cassidy said. "I need to talk to Rhy about getting a search warrant. It's a long shot. I'm not sure seeing his vehicle last night and having him on the same gaming site as Travis—along with a million other users—will be enough."

"Try ten million users and more jumping on the site every day," he said. The way some facts popped into his mind was a little annoying. He needed to know what he and Travis had been concerned about regarding the Sorcerer's Sword game.

"I wonder if my stepsiblings Ben and Brian Hamilton are on there." She waved a hand at his computer screen. "I assume so as they are big into computer games." Was there a hint of derision in her tone?

He told himself not to overact. He performed a quick search and nodded. "Yep, both of them are."

Her brow furrowed. "Do you think they're in danger?"

"I doubt it," he hastened to assure her. "They took Travis and have targeted me for a reason. I don't think other users are at risk." Yet as he said the words, he noticed both were discussing the merits of the game and their plans to purchase it. Was he wrong about the danger? He prayed he wasn't. He noticed another user with the code name Axe had attacked Travis's post about the security, claiming it was ridiculous.

"You're probably right." She shook her head. "Honestly, I'm still trying to understand why any game would cause gunmen to find and try to kill you."

"I agree, it doesn't make sense. But I'm sure we'll know more once we find Travis." That gave him a thought. He pulled up another program and did a search on Miles Wayland.

"What program are you using? I don't think I have access to it," Cassidy said with a frown.

"Yeah, you wouldn't," he said absently. He nodded with satisfaction when he found what he was looking for. "Here, these are Miles's parents, Gordan and Joanna Wayland. Now I'll run a property search on them." As he spoke, his fingers played the keyboard. It took a minute for the results to bloom on the page.

Again, Cassidy leaned over his shoulder, so close he could turn his head and kiss her. He forced himself to focus on the screen. "They own a house in Brookland, which is interesting. And they own a small house on Newport Lake. It's a much smaller lake than Peabody Lake or the other more popular lakes nearby. But it's also not far, only thirty minutes from their home in Brookland."

"Good to know," Cassidy said. "I think we should get out to the lake house to see if Travis is there. First, I need to call Rhy to fill him in."

He nodded in understanding. The hour was barely six, but with a pregnant wife and small child, their boss would likely be up. And it would be good to know if they were able to get the search warrant. If not, they could still head out to search for Travis, but they'd be trespassing on private property.

Not that he cared about breaking that law. Gaming was a connection between Miles and Travis, and they saw Miles's SUV near the restaurant where they'd found the phone used to call his desk. In his mind, that was more than enough to take action.

Lawyers could take a long walk off a short pier, he thought darkly. His brother's life was at stake. He wasn't going to stand around and wait for the slow wheel of justice to turn in his favor.

"Yeah, sure Rhy. We'll wait for you to get here." Cassidy sent him an apologetic look. "Talk soon." She ended the call.

"We're wasting time," he said. "We need to get to that lake house."

"And we will," she assured him. "But Rhy wants to see if we can get a judge to approve the search warrant first."

He shook his head and rose to his feet. "Sorry, Cass, but I'm not waiting. They could be on the move again in the daylight. If the place is empty, then there's no point in getting a search warrant."

She held his gaze for a long moment then slowly nodded. "I see your point. But I need a few minutes. I think we need one more cop to ride along in case we're outnumbered."

He swallowed his protest and nodded. Finding Travis was important but so was keeping Cassidy safe. "We'll take our vests too," he said, reaching for the one he'd worn a few hours ago.

"Hey, Jina, do you have time to run down a lead on Gabe's missing brother?" Cassidy listened for a moment, then said, "Great. You're closer to Newport Lake than we are, so meet us there in say thirty minutes. Wear your tactical gear since we don't know what we're walking into. Thanks." She lowered the phone. "Let's go before Rhy can stop us."

He hated putting her career in jeopardy, but that didn't stop him from shrugging into his coat, tugging it over the vest. Then he picked up the laptop, for no other reason than he felt naked without it. "I'm ready."

She nodded, having already donned her vest and jacket. They quickly headed toward the side exit. He didn't realize he was holding his breath until they reached the rental vehicle. He sighed and snapped the seat belt into place, relieved they'd gotten away clean.

Cass didn't say much. The hour was early enough that they weren't hampered by rush-hour traffic. He wanted to keep looking through the gaming software but decided to rest his eyes and his injured brain.

Please, Lord Jesus, restore my memory! Guide us to Travis and keep him safe in Your care.

A sense of peace washed over him. Praying came more naturally now, either because of Cassidy's influence or because he'd attended church prior to his concussion. Either way, he needed every ounce of the Lord's support and comfort now more than ever.

"When we find Travis, I'd like you to give him the benefit of doubt," he said, breaking the silence. "He may have started off as a willing accomplice, but his phone call indicates he's in trouble."

"Of course." She shot him a sideways glance. "We don't arrest people willy-nilly. We need probable cause. Besides Travis is underage and has been reported missing by his mother. Unless he pulls a gun and shoots at us, there's no reason to arrest him."

"Thanks." He couldn't imagine Travis shooting at them, but he also wasn't sure what this was about. As Cassidy had pointed out several times, it made no sense why anyone kill him over a video game.

Twenty-five minutes later, he saw the sign for Newport Lake. He straightened in his seat and eyed the addresses. "We're getting close," he said as they passed mailboxes perched on the end of driveways. "There! That's the one."

Cass glanced at the small brown cottage associated with the address he'd provided. She drove past the place, which didn't surprise him. Three houses down, she pulled over and parked. "I didn't see a car in the driveway, did you?"

"No. But there is a garage, could be that the blue SUV belonging to Miles is parked inside." He unlatched his seat-belt. "Your plan is to approach the place on foot?"

"Yes, but you need to stay here." Cassidy shut off the engine. "Jina and I will go up to the door."

"Travis is my brother," he protested, but Cassidy pierced him with a narrow look.

"Nonnegotiable, Gabe. If you don't stay here, then I'll drive back to the precinct to wait for a warrant."

A warrant they may not get. Frustrated, he grudgingly nodded. "Okay, fine. I'll stay here." What he didn't add was that if he heard any sounds of trouble, like gunshots, he'd be out of the car and on scene faster than she could blink.

"I mean it," she said, sliding out from behind the wheel. "Rhy will kill me if anything happens to you."

Annoyed, he scowled but stayed in his seat. He took note of the time, six-forty-two in the morning. He decided he'd give her a solid fifteen minutes before bailing on his promise and heading out to join her and Jina.

It would be the longest fifteen minutes of his life.

CASS WAS glad the sky was overcast and that the sun wouldn't rise for another thirty minutes or so. This close to the winter solstice meant long nights and short days.

A fact that worked in her favor.

As she headed toward the brown cabin, she paused when she saw headlights growing brighter as a vehicle approached. Lifting a hand to ward off the brightness, she relaxed when she recognized Jina's SUV.

Her teammate pulled off to the side of the road and lowered her window. "See anything yet?"

"No car in the driveway," Cass confirmed. "It's that brown house up ahead."

"I'm ready." Jina raised the window and shut down the car. She slid out and quickly joined Cass. "You really think Travis is being held here?"

"There's only one way to find out." Cass gestured toward the driveway. "Let's not take the direct approach yet. I'd rather we split up and get close to the house, see if anyone is inside."

"Works for me." Jina grinned, never one to be afraid of a confrontation. "I'll take the east; you take the west."

Cass nodded, and they quickly broke apart to head off in opposite directions.

There was some foliage along the sides of the driveway, which helped keep her in the shadows. She held her service weapon ready as she covered the distance to the house. There she paused, giving Jina time to get in position.

She didn't see any lights on inside, but it was also early. Her stepbrothers slept till noon on weekends, and if Miles and Travis had been out at the restaurant last night, they were likely still sound asleep.

The garage was on Jina's side, so she didn't have a chance to look inside. She kept her attention focused on the windows lining the side of the house closest to her. Beyond that, she caught a glimpse of the serene lake. The water along the shoreline was iced over, but the weather hadn't been cold enough to freeze the deeper areas. That would come in January and February, she knew.

The first window she reached was a bedroom. Disappointed to find it was covered with curtains, she moved onto the next. That was also covered, so she crept to the front corner of the house. Surely the windows facing the lake would not be shrouded in drapes.

She peered around the corner to the backyard. On the opposite side of the small home, she saw Jina doing the same.

Her colleague shook her head, indicating she hadn't seen anyone. Cass shook her head too, then eased around the corner to sidle up to the next window. As she'd anticipated, this one did not have curtains pulled across the opening. She scanned the interior, but unlike the mess at the restaurant, there were no empty wrappers or dirty dishes lying around.

On the other side, Jina was approaching the window closest to her. Then she gestured for Cass to join her.

Bending at the waist to avoid being seen, she moved quickly to Jina's side.

"Looks like computer gaming devices on the living room table," Jina whispered in her ear.

Cass nodded, seeing them for herself. The handheld gaming controls weren't necessarily proof that Travis and Miles were inside. Still, she felt certain they had been there, and recently.

"Did you see an SUV in the garage?" she asked in a low voice

"Negative," Jina whispered back. "It's empty."

She pursed her lips, realizing Miles and Travis must not have come back here for the night, as she'd hoped. "What do you think? Should we go back to the front and announce ourselves? We don't have probable cause to break in."

"Can't hurt," Jina agreed with a shrug. "Right behind you."

Cass took the lead, going around the corner to reach the front of the property. As she passed by the windows, she noted that like the others there were curtains covering the opening. The boys could have ditched the SUV somewhere close and walked there, but it didn't seem likely.

As she approached the front door, twin headlights cut through the darkness. On instinct, she and Jina turned and darted back to the far east side of the property, seeking cover behind the garage.

The lights drove past, likely someone heading to the day job. She felt foolish for overreacting, but Jina patted her shoulder.

"Time for take two," her friend whispered in a teasing tone.

She offered a rueful smile and waited for the lights to dim in the distance, before heading back out to the front yard. In silent agreement, she stood to one side of the door while Jina took the other. More than once, bad guys had fired through doors to deter cops from coming inside.

At close range, a bullet to the chest even while wearing a vest could be deadly.

She knocked sharply on the door. "Miles Wayland? We're with the police! I need you to open the door and come out with your hands up over your head!"

There was nothing but silence. She hadn't heard any movement from inside, but the cottage could be well insulated.

She tried again. "Police! Open the door and come out with your hands up!"

Still nothing. Her shoulders slumped as she glanced at Jina. Her friend shrugged, indicating there wasn't much more they could do.

Cass was about to try one last time when another pair of headlights pierced the early morning darkness. Newport Lake was far enough from the bigger cities that the ambient light was much less than what she was used to.

She hesitated, unwilling to look foolish, but Jina reached out, grabbed her arm, and tugged. Following the wordless command, she darted across the front yard to once again seek refuge behind the garage.

The lights grew brighter, and she found herself holding her breath as they did not pass by. Instead, she heard the low rumble of the garage door opening.

She frowned at Jina, who looked just as surprised as she was by the unexpected arrival of either Miles, Travis and others, or the property owners themselves.

She and Jina waited for long seconds as the car pulled into the garage. Only once the garage door closed did she lean forward to whisper, "I think we should check the windows again. I need to know if Travis is inside."

Jina nodded and gestured to the side of the house. "You stay here. I'll go around to the other side."

She nodded and moved forward along the side of the house. None of the windows were lit up from the inside, but as she reached the corner of the house that overlooked the lake, it was easy to see someone had entered the living room and kitchen areas.

In three steps, she was at the window peering in. She saw a tall skinny guy with dark hair standing with his back to the window. He gestured wildly, as if arguing over something.

Or someone?

She pictured Miles Wayland's driver's license photo in her mind. Long, shaggy dark hair, tall and thin. That had to be him, although it was hard to say for sure with his back to her.

Ducking so that she was below the windowsill, she quickly moved to the next window, desperate to see if Travis was there too.

Taking a deep breath, she edged closer and took a quick look. To her disappointment, she saw an older man, not Travis.

Miles's father? Or someone else?

She glanced at Jina who held her hands palm up as if to say, *Your call on our next steps*. There was no way to know if Travis was being held at another location or if Miles Wayland wasn't involved at all.

No, her gut told her they were on the right track. She bent so as not to be seen from those inside and ran toward Jina.

"Let's go knock again," she said. "We know for sure they're home."

"I'm in," Jina said with a nod.

Less than a minute later, she was back on the front porch, standing off to the side as Jina did the same. She hadn't seen a weapon in the occupant's hands, but that didn't mean they weren't armed.

"Police!" Cass shouted as she pounded on the door. "Open up! We're looking for Miles Wayland!"

From the corner of her eye, she saw Gabe running toward them. She scowled and waved him back as the porch light flicked on, and the front door opened. It was the older man who stood there, his expression pulled into a scowl.

"What do you want?" he demanded, speaking through the screen door. "Let me see your badge!"

Cass pulled hers out and showed it to him. Jina did the same thing. "Are you Gordon Wayland? We need to speak to your son, Miles." When the older man hesitated, she quickly added, "Don't lie to us, sir. We know Miles is here because we saw him inside. We're not leaving until we talk to him."

The older man scowled, then stepped back. "Miles," he called in a resigned tone. "You better talk to them."

Cassidy slipped her badge back into her pocket, readying herself in case the kid decided to run. He wouldn't get far, but she really hated it when the perps made her chase after them. It was a surefire way for one or both of them to get injured.

"What?" The tall skinny man with dark shaggy hair sidled up to the door, his expression a mixture of anger, anxiety, and fear.

Good, she thought with a surge of satisfaction. He should be wary if he's involved in this. "Miles Wayland?"

she asked. When he reluctantly nodded, she said, "Please step outside. We have a few questions for you."

"Why? Am I under arrest?" His tone was sulky, as if he was being grounded from playing video games.

She arched a brow. "I don't know, should you be? We need to know the whereabouts of a missing teenager. And we know you were in communication with him."

Miles stiffened, then said. "I don't know anything about Travis. And if I'm not under arrest, I don't have to talk to you."

"Wrong answer, Miles," Jina drawled. "You admitted to knowing Travis, and that gives us probable cause to arrest you."

Cass pulled open the screen door, and thankfully, Miles wasn't quick enough to stop her. Elbowing the door aside, she reached out and grabbed his arm. Yanking hard, she pulled him down onto the porch. "Miles Wayland, you're under arrest for endangering the welfare of a minor. You have the right to remain silent. Anything you say can and will be used against you in a court of law." She pushed his lean frame up against the side of the house, waiting for Jina to bring her handcuffs over to secure his wrists. "You have the right to an attorney. If you cannot afford one, an attorney will be provided at no cost to you."

"Hey, wait!" the older man protested. "You can't do that. I'm his father, you can't just take him away."

"Mr. Wayland, Miles is an adult, and therefore, you have no say over the matter." She eyed him thoughtfully. "Unless you're involved in Travis's disappearance too?"

"Of course not," Gordon denied hotly. "This is ridiculous. Miles, don't say anything until I can hire a lawyer."

"Mr. Wayland, we need to make sure Travis isn't in the house, the garage, or the car." Cassidy kept her voice firm, not asking for permission so much as telling him what she wanted.

"Go ahead," Gordon said, throwing his hands out. "He's not here. We just arrived ourselves."

The grimace on Miles's face told her he might know more than he's letting on. She pushed him toward Jina and then headed inside.

The search didn't take long. The place was empty. If Travis had been there, he wasn't any longer.

She caught Gabe's agonized expression when she returned without his brother. She felt bad for him, knowing that they needed to convince Miles to talk if they had any hope of finding Travis.

CHAPTER THIRTEEN

When Cass emerged from the house without his brother, a flash of anger hit hard. They'd come too far to leave empty-handed. Miles Wayland had to know where Travis was!

Gabe rushed forward, grabbing the kid's shoulders and shaking him. "Where's Travis? You need to tell me where he is!"

"Easy, Gabe," Jina cautioned. "We'll get him to talk."

"Tell me where he is!" He shook the kid again, unable to hide his panicked distress. "Did you kill him? Is that it? Did you kill a seventeen-year-old kid?"

"No, no, no," Miles stuttered. "No!"

"Hey, get him away from my son!" Gordon Wayland shouted from the doorway. "That's police brutality! Let him go or I'll file a complaint with the Newport Police Department."

Police brutality would be if Gabe punched the kid in the jaw, which was tempting, but he managed to hold back. Nobody bothered to correct Gordon's assumption that they were local police. He released Miles's shoulders but didn't back off.

"Mr. Wayland, I highly advise you convince your son to cooperate with us," Cassidy said in a calm but firm tone. "If Travis McCord is dead, your son will face serious charges. First degree murder and kidnapping a minor, and those are just for starters. A young man's life is at stake."

"My son didn't kill anyone!" Gordon shot back. But when Miles fell silent, standing with his head down and his shoulders slumped in defeat, his father frowned, and said, "Miles? You don't know this Travis kid, do you?"

When Miles didn't immediately answer, Gordon strode purposefully from the house, planting himself in front of his son. Gabe took two steps back, praying Gordon would convince Miles to cooperate.

"Miles?" Gordon glared at him. "I asked you a question."

More silence.

"If you know something about this missing kid, you need to tell us," Jina said as father and son simply stared at each other. "Every minute counts. If you don't cooperate, and we find that Travis has been killed, you will face murder charges."

Gabe noticed Miles went pale upon hearing that.

"However, if you talk to us now, I'll let the DA's office know that you cooperated with the investigation," Cass added. "But if you don't, then you'll face the consequences of your actions in front of a judge."

"Miles, please." Gordon's voice was low and urgent. His earlier claims regarding his son's innocence had vanished as the older man seemed to understand Miles knew far more than he was letting on. "Tell them the truth. I know you wouldn't hurt anyone. Don't stand there and take the fall for someone else's actions."

"I don't know where they took him," Miles finally said. "Travis should have just kept his mouth shut."

Gabe's stomach knotted. "Who took him? Tell us their names."

Miles opened his mouth to answer, but Gordon quickly interrupted. "Wait, I want assurances that you won't press charges against Miles if he cooperates."

Gabe would have instantly agreed but noticed that Jina and Cassidy exchanged a long look. "I have to run that past the DA's office," Cass finally said. "Your ability to get a deal depends on the extent of your involvement in the crime."

"He's not talking until we meet with the DA," Gordon repeated. "I don't want Miles to face any charges."

"Fine, then we'll take Miles to the precinct," Jina said with a shrug.

Gordon started to protest, but Cassidy interrupted him. "We'll talk to the DA's office on the way back to Milwaukee. I'm sure we can arrange for one of the ADAs to join us in the interview."

No! Gabe didn't want to wait a second longer than necessary. Miles made it sound as if Travis was still alive the last time he saw him, but that was hours ago.

The men who had him may have already killed him.

"We'll find him," Cass murmured as Jina marched the cuffed Miles toward her SUV. "We're one step closer Gabe. This kid will tell us what we need to know."

"What if it's too late?" He searched her gaze as dawn crept over the horizon. "What if they've gotten rid of Travis by now?"

"Gabe, I know this is incredibly difficult." She wrapped her arm around his waist, hugging him close. "I won't lie to you. It is possible they've killed Travis. It's been several hours since they went on the run. But they've kept him alive this long for a reason. We need to stay positive. To have faith in God's plan."

He wasn't sure he could do that, but he managed to nod. Everything she said was true. It had been hours since they'd found the phone in the restaurant. If they wanted to silence his brother, they'd have had plenty of time to do the job.

And if they hadn't? He glared at Miles as he slid into the back of Jina's SUV. "You need to get answers from him, Cass. And soon."

"That's the goal." She hugged him again. "Let's hit the road. I'll make some calls along the way."

"Where are you taking Miles?" Gordon asked. "I thought you were from the Newport police station."

"We're MPD," she said. Then she rattled off the address of the Seventh Precinct police station. Gabe felt a flash of sympathy for the older man. Gordon Wayland looked as if he'd aged ten years since they'd arrived.

"Thank you. I'll be there soon." Gordon turned and headed back inside the cabin.

As he followed Cass back to their SUV, he asked, "Will you let Miles's father participate in the interview?"

She shrugged. "By law, we don't have to. But if Gordan can get his son to cooperate, I'm all for it."

"Me too," Gabe murmured.

"Are you able to drive?" Cassidy asked as they neared the rental. She pulled the key fob from her pocket and tossed it to him.

"Yes." He gratefully took the key, knowing she'd get more work done on the trip back than he would.

They were back on the road and heading toward the interstate a few minutes later. True to her word, Cassidy made several calls. He listened to her side of the conversation as he drove. "Hey, Rhy, Jina is bringing in a suspect by the name of Miles Wayland to the precinct. We believe he has pertinent information regarding the disappearance of Travis McCord."

If Rhy was upset about them leaving before he arrived, Cassidy's expression didn't let on.

He listened as she described how they'd tracked Miles Wayland to the cottage on Newport Lake. "We were checking the place out when Miles Wayland and his father, Gordon, arrived home. They weren't cooperative at first, but once we arrested Miles, he pretty much intimated that he knew Travis but didn't know where they had taken him." A pause, then, "No, he didn't say who *they* were. His dad stopped him, demanding a deal in exchange for his son's cooperation with the investigation. My next call is to your brother-in-law Bax Scala to hopefully make that happen."

Gabe pushed the speed limit, but the flash of brake lights up ahead made him groan. Of course, they were heading downtown right during rush hour.

"The one comment Miles did let slip was that Travis should have kept his mouth shut. I'm not sure if that's related to the secret call he made to Gabe's office from the disposable phone, or something else entirely."

He had found that comment from Miles interesting too. It could have been in reference to the phone call, but Gabe couldn't help but wonder if it was more than that. Like the fact that Travis had reached out to him in the first place about the gaming software. Prior to his being assaulted.

He hit the brake, slowing as traffic became more congested. At this rate, it would take twice as long to get back to the precinct as it had for them to get to Newport Lake.

It took a minute for him to realize Cass was onto the next call to Bax Scala. That conversation was short, and it sounded as if Bax was more than willing to meet them at the precinct.

"Everything set?" he asked when Cass lowered her phone.

"Yes, thankfully, Bax didn't have court this morning, so he was able to rearrange his schedule for this." She glanced at him. "We're close, Gabe. Very close."

He wished he shared her confidence, but until he could see Travis for himself, he found it difficult to believe. Losing his memory had limited their ability to work the case.

His gut clenched at the thought of facing his mother if they didn't find Travis in time to save him.

"This is not your fault," Cassidy said, reading his expression. "The responsibility lies with the bad guys. Not you."

"Maybe." He felt certain he had played a key role in this mess. And that the guilt would be worse once his memory returned.

A painstaking fifteen minutes later, he was able to exit the interstate. The traffic lights were in his favor as he navigated the streets to the precinct. He was surprised to see that Jina and Miles had just arrived as well.

The four of them walked into the precinct, Cass and Jina keeping Miles between them. Rhy came out to meet them, gesturing to the open interview room.

"Has he been read his rights?" Rhy asked.

"Yes, sir," Jina and Cass replied in unison. "Miles's father is on his way. Gordon Wayland requested the DA's office to be present to make a deal."

Rhy frowned. "Is this Gordon a lawyer?"

"I don't think so," Jina said. "He originally said he'd get a lawyer, but once he realized Miles knew more than he was telling us, he changed his tune to getting a deal."

With a grimace, Rhy nodded. "It's up to Bax how he wants to proceed." Rhy met Gabe's gaze. "It may be that we have to wait for a lawyer to represent Wayland."

Swallowing hard, he forced a nod. "I understand. But the bad guys know that Travis reached out to me. It's critical we find Travis as soon as possible."

"We'll find him," Rhy said, echoing Cassidy's earlier words. "You can watch the interview from the anteroom."

It was another blow to know he wouldn't be allowed in the interview room with Miles and his father.

All he could do now was to wait, listen, and pray.

CASSIDY FELT the anguish reflected in Gabe's eyes all the way down to her soul. There were times, like now, when all cops chafed against the constraints of the legal system.

Obviously, the goal was to protect the innocent. A few months ago, when Jina had been a murder suspect, the rules had been helpful. But eyeing Miles slouched in his chair, with his stringy hair hanging in his face, she doubted he was an innocent bystander in this.

She grabbed a water bottle from the fridge and headed into the conference room. She offered it to Miles, who gratefully took it.

"ADA Bax Scala will be joining us soon," she said as she took the seat next to the young man. "You need to understand you are being recorded. When ADA Scala gets here, he'll outline the terms of the proposed agreement."

Miles finally lifted his head. "Can my dad be here with me?"

She glanced at Jina, who shrugged. "That will be up to ADA Scala."

As if on cue, the door opened. Bax strode in, sharply dressed in what was probably a thousand-dollar hand-tailored suit, followed by a very anxious-looking Gordon Wayland. "Miles Wayland? I'm Assistant District Attorney Scala. I understand you're requesting your father sit in on this interview for support and guidance in lieu of an attorney." When Miles blinked, Bax said, "Is that correct?"

"Yes. I want my dad, not an attorney."

Bax gave a nod. "And you also understand this interview is being recorded?"

"Yes." Miles sent a furtive look toward his father. "I don't want to do any jail time."

Bax sat directly across from Miles and his father. He held the young man's gaze. "I'm willing to work with you, Miles, but you need to give me something that indicates you're negotiating in good faith." Again, Miles looked blank, so Bax clarified further, "I mean you need to give me some information that lets me know you're willing to cooperate." Bax leaned forward. "Is Travis McCord still alive?"

Miles grimaced. "He was the last time I saw him."

"And when was that?" Bax pressed.

"I dunno. Two thirty or three this morning?" Miles made it sound like a question rather than an answer.

"Miles, I need direct answers to my questions. If you can't help me, there's no reason for me to make a deal regarding minimal to no jail time." Bax was clearly getting annoyed. "Either you're here to cooperate or you aren't."

"Miles, answer his questions." Gordon nudged his son with his elbow. "Tell them about this kid Travis."

"The last time I saw Travis he was being driven away in a van from the Homerun Restaurant and Bar. I can't tell you the exact time, but it was somewhere between two thirty and three in the morning. The minute Turk found out that Travis made a phone call, they hustled him outta there."

Bax nodded slowly. "Okay, so you know the men who have Travis. Is that correct?"

Miles lifted a bony shoulder. "Yeah, I know their names."

"Okay, then. I will agree to dropping all charges against you in exchange for detailed information about who these men are and why they took Travis." Bax spoke plainly enough for Miles to understand.

The kid glanced at his father, then nodded. "Okay."

"One more thing," Bax said with an intense gaze. "If we discover you lied to us at any point during the remainder of this investigation, this deal is null and void. Do you understand? If you lie, I will prosecute you to the fullest extent of the law."

"Yeah, yeah." Miles hunched his shoulders again. "I hear you. No lying."

Cass was impressed with how well Bax was managing the situation but could sense Gabe's impatience radiating through the one-way glass. She sent a reassuring smile, even though she couldn't see him.

"Who is Turk, and why does he have Travis?" Bax asked.

"I dunno his first name; the guys call him Turk, which I learned was shorthand for Turkow," Miles said. "He's the guy in charge. They took Travis because he discovered the hidden spyware in the Sorcerer's Sword software."

"Spyware?" Cassidy asked with a frown. "You mean the goal is to spy on the general public through the game?"

"Not like, to see them or anything," Miles said. "There isn't a camera. But the spyware will infiltrate the computer network giving them access to all online banking information." Miles shrugged again. "They claim they'll be rich in a matter of weeks, once the holiday is over and every kid across the world with money to burn has started to play the game."

Cassidy glanced toward the one-way mirror again, imagining Gabe's reaction to hearing this. They shouldn't have been surprised to learn the root of this nightmare was money. Greed was the motive of most crimes. She knew he'd be upset that he hadn't figured out the spyware aspect to the software he'd downloaded to the USB drive, but they had what they needed now. At least in part. They still needed to find Travis.

She turned back to face Miles. "Okay, you don't know Turkow's first name, but you must know the names of the others involved in this," she said reasonably. "Start with how many guys were at the Homerun bar earlier this morning? You, Travis, and who else?"

"Three others. Turk, Lonny, and King."

She frowned. "That's not good enough. Those sound like screen names, not legal names. We need to be able to track these guys down."

"I don't know their real names," Miles's voice turned whiny. "We're gamers. That's how we know each other."

This wasn't nearly as helpful as she'd hoped. She glanced at Jina, feeling helpless. How could they possibly find these guys based on names like Turk, Lonny, and King? She turned her attention back to Miles. "Think back to the time you spent with them. You heard Turkow's full name, right? Maybe you heard something else? Maybe Lonny stands for Lionel? And King is either a first or a last name?"

"Maybe." Miles glanced at his father who was starting to look sick to his stomach at what his son was revealing. "My screen name is Millions. Because you know, that's the end goal. To make millions so I don't have to work at some dead-end job."

It was all she could do not to laugh, cry, or scream with frustration. Based on the incredulous expression on Gordon's face, his father felt the same way.

"You mentioned they took Travis in a van," Jina said, turning the conversation back to the facts at hand. "What kind of van? A box van without windows? Or a minivan? We need the make, model, and license plate number."

"Dark-gray minivan, I think it's a Ford." Miles did not sound at all confident. "I didn't pay attention to the license plate. But if it helps, the Turk always drives the van. He doesn't let anyone else get behind the wheel."

"We can work on finding dark-gray vans that belong to someone with the last name of Turkow," Cassidy said. "Is there anything else specific about the van? Dents or stickers of any kind?"

"Not that I remember," Miles said. His expression was earnest as if he'd taken the threat about not lying to heart. "I didn't pay any attention to that kind of stuff, you know?"

"What did you focus on?" Jina asked.

"The game." Miles's eyes gleamed with interest. For the first time since picking him up at the lake house, the kid came alive. Which was a little sad when she thought about it. A bit like Ben and Brian whose whole world revolved around games. "The game was the best thing to hit the market in years. Everyone had been talking about it for weeks prior to its release last week. Stores were selling out the minute stock hit the shelves." Miles waved a hand. "I work at the Game and Go store, so I got to see it before anyone else. The graphics are phenomenal, and the levels are super hard."

"How exactly did you get involved with Turkow and

the others?" Bax asked when Miles took a breath. She sensed the kid would have kept going on and on about the stupid game without taking into consideration the fact that Travis's life was at risk because of it.

The blunt question caused Miles to deflate. He stared down at the table for a long moment, avoiding his father's gaze. "I connected with them on Dorian."

At Bax's confused expression, she said, "That's a social media site for gamers."

Bax nodded. "Okay. Go on."

Miles swallowed hard, still avoiding his father's gaze. "There were rumblings about this game making people rich. Like I said, Travis is a big name on Dorian, he's wicked smart. Beats every game faster than anyone else, and there are a lot of gamers who resent him for that." Miles paused, then said, "Travis bragged that he knew exactly how the game was being used to make money and that he was taking care of it." Miles shrugged, then said, "After he made that post, he went silent on the site."

Cassidy nodded as some of the puzzle pieces fell into place. "That explains why Travis was kidnapped, but we still need to understand how you got involved. Why were you at the Homerun bar?"

"Turk is a friend of mine," Miles finally admitted. "We go way back to when Dorian was a relatively new site for gamers. He messaged me privately and said it was urgent that we get to Travis before he could ruin it for everyone. He said the game was incredible, and Travis didn't know what he was talking about."

"Wait a minute." Cassidy held up a hand. "That doesn't make sense. If Travis didn't know what he was talking about, then there was no threat. No reason for you to get to Travis before he could ruin it."

"Yeah, I said that to the Turk," Miles admitted. "After a few messages back and forth, the Turk finally admitted the money-making scheme was for real and that he would make it worth my while to help him out." He hesitated, then said, "I knew Travis from the Game and Go store. We shared screen names so we could play each other. I have to admit, he kicked my butt every single time."

"Back to the money," Cass pressed.

"Yeah, well, the Turk said we couldn't discuss it online, only in person." Miles still didn't look at his father. "So I went out to meet with him."

"How much did he offer you?" Bax asked. Cass wondered if he was regretting making the deal now that he knew exactly what was involved.

"Five hundred thousand dollars." Jina gaped in shock, but Cass tried to keep her expression neutral. "He convinced me I would be halfway to my million-dollar goal if I helped them out. So I, uh, agreed to bring Travis to meet Turk." Miles finally looked up from the table, his gaze beseeching. "I swear I had no idea that Turk and his buddies intended to hurt anyone. I didn't even know that the spyware was inserted into the software to illegally access their bank accounts."

"What did you think?" Gordon suddenly demanded. He took them all by surprise when he cuffed his son on the back of his head. "You didn't think at all, did you? How many times do I have to tell you that there's no easy way to make money? Nobody gets rich sitting on their butt playing stupid games. The only way to get ahead in this world is by working hard! A concept you can't seem to comprehend."

Miles hung his head, looking miserable.

"Okay, so you agreed to bring Travis to Turkow," Cassidy said, getting them back on track. "Where did that meeting take place? Who was there, and which one of you hit Gabe Melrose in the head?"

Before Miles could answer, the interview room door burst open. Gabe rushed in, holding a laptop in his arms. The fact that Rhy hadn't stopped him indicated he'd uncovered key intel to the case.

"Is this Turkow?" Gabe dropped the machine in front of Miles. "Is that the guy who has Travis?"

"Yeah, that's the Turk," Miles admitted. "I didn't know his first name was David, but that's him."

Gabe lifted his gaze to hers. "I found him via the intel on the van. Now that we have a positive ID, I'll run a search on all known properties. From there, we should be able to get a search warrant."

"Go for it," she said. "Get what we need. I'll join you as soon as we're finished here."

She sensed Gabe wanted to argue, but he turned away without saying anything. A surge of satisfaction hit hard.

They had a viable lead. She felt certain that David Turkow would lead them directly to Travis.

Please, Lord Jesus, keep Travis safe in Your care!

CHAPTER FOURTEEN

It didn't take long to search for property belonging to David Turkow. Not only did Gabe discover the guy's father owned the Homerun Restaurant and Bar that was currently listed for sale, but Scott Turkow also owned a warehouse that wasn't far from the location where he'd been dumped the night he'd sustained his head injury.

Using the map application, Gabe zoomed in on the building. Seeing the warehouse up close brought a cascade of memories.

He remembered being there that fateful night. Earlier that week, he and Travis had been in contact about the Sorcerer's Sword game. His brother had identified the anomaly, and they'd worked together to uncover and identify the malware. Gabe's plan was to take the information to the feds the following morning, but later that night, Travis had called in a panic claiming he was in danger and asked Gabe to meet him with the information regarding the game's operating system. Suspicious, Gabe had instead hidden the USB drive in his freezer, then called for a rideshare to head out to meet his brother.

Then Travis had called again, saying not to come because it was a trap. Gabe had ignored the warning since he was already near their designated meeting spot. He'd been glad to see Travis's blue Corvette parked in front of the warehouse. He'd intended to sneak up to see what was going on when he'd been ambushed. A group of men had rushed out of the building. One, no, two including Miles had held Travis back while the other two hit him with a brick. The last thing he remembered was Travis's panicked expression.

A chill snaked down Gabe's spine as he remembered how scared Travis had been. Like fearing his life was over for good scared. The past twenty-four hours proved these guys were ruthless. He understood now that they knew he'd retained a copy of the malware. They'd searched him, taken his phone, wallet, and everything he had on him. But he hadn't brought the USB drive, and his foresight in hiding it had put a crimp in their plan. He suspected they hadn't killed him that first night because they figured they'd find the USB drive in his house and would grab it and be done.

Except they hadn't found it in the freezer.

With an abrupt movement, he pushed away from the computer, snagged the USB drive along with his coat, and left the precinct through the side door.

Rhy, Cassidy, and the others would be angry with him, but he needed to do this. His mother was right in that the situation was his fault. He needed to find Travis. The bad guys were armed and dangerous, and he feared a full-on gunfight would ensue if he couldn't figure out a way to smooth things over. Besides, he had the malware as a bargaining chip.

Gabe still had the key fob to the rental. He slid in behind the wheel, started the engine, and shot out of the parking lot. In the rearview mirror, he caught a hint of movement and realized Cassidy and Rhy had come out of the building to stare after him in shock.

It was tempting to turn around, as he hated disappointing the two people who meant the most to him. Especially Cassidy.

But he didn't. Instead, he tightened his grip on the steering wheel and pushed his foot down hard on the accelerator. They would likely follow him, he'd left the map up on his computer screen, so he didn't have time to waste. He needed to get Travis out of the warehouse.

If that was where he was being held.

He felt certain that was where they were. The morning rush-hour traffic had thinned. He made good time heading out of the city.

As he drove, he tried to come up with a viable plan. This part of the job wasn't his area of expertise. He didn't think like a cop, but he was still wearing the tactical gear Cassidy had given him. He decided he could offer himself up in exchange for Travis.

He wondered how much it would hurt to be hit in the chest with a bullet at close range, then pushed the concern out of his mind.

It didn't matter. Anything to get Travis out of there.

He took the exit that would lead to the warehouse. Instead of driving there, though, he pulled the rental off the road in the area where he'd woken up, dazed and concussed. No doubt Cassidy and the rest of the team would be able to track the car to this location.

Bailing out of the vehicle, he zipped his coat over the vest and made sure the USB drive was tucked deep into his pocket. He drew in a deep breath, glanced up at the overcast sky, then approached the warehouse from the back.

The way he should have that fateful night.

When the warehouse came into view, his gut clenched with dread. Logically, he knew he could be walking to his death.

He wished he'd told Cassidy how much he loved her. Then he reminded himself that God was watching over them.

Please, Lord, guide me to Travis! Grant me the strength to rescue him!

Again, the prayers brought a sense of calm washing over him. There was nothing to fear. Regret? Yes, especially concerning Cassidy. But he would not be afraid.

There was only a small rear door along the back of the warehouse. He glanced around, wondering if there were cameras hidden in the eaves. He didn't see any, so he lightly ran to the door and tried the knob.

It wasn't locked.

A trap? He felt certain the door must have been left open on purpose, but what choice did he have? Stand around out there or go inside.

He stood to the side, pressing his back against the wall of the building, and opened the door awkwardly with one hand. He made sure to only open it an inch, yet he fully expected the three men to rush him.

Nothing happened.

He moved closer, peering through the narrow opening. It wasn't easy to see; there were no lights inside. His heart sank as he opened the door a little farther to see better. Was the warehouse empty? Had he picked the wrong location?

The back of the warehouse was full of boxes. He caught a glimpse of a wall stretching across the space and realized there was a front part to the warehouse as well.

The thud of footsteps made him freeze for a moment.

Then without giving himself a chance to think it through, he slipped through the opening and quickly closed the door behind him, plunging the back portion of the warehouse into darkness.

"I heard something," a voice said.

"You're delirious," another person responded. "No one knows we're here."

Two men for sure, but there was likely a third. What had Miles said? Turk, Lonny, and King.

Wishing he'd thought to snag a weapon, he moved as silently as possible through the boxes toward the opening that led to the front area of the warehouse. He desperately needed to see Travis was still alive and relatively unharmed before he made his next move.

"How long are you going to keep me here?" Gabe's heart swelled with relief when he heard Travis's voice. "I told you I don't have the malware. Killing me will only set you up for being charged with murder."

Gabe silently urged Travis to keep talking as he edged closer to the opening.

"We need to do something," a third whiny voice said. "We can't trust Millions to keep his trap shut."

"We need that USB drive," the first voice snapped. "Train here is going to get that for us, understand?"

Gabe knew Train was Travis's screen name. How exactly did these guys expect Travis to get the USB drive? They probably had a plan, one he hoped to derail in a big way.

He tried to gauge how long it had been since he'd left the precinct. Twenty minutes? Thirty?

If he were honest, he'd secretly hoped Cassidy and Rhy would come to the rescue. He shouldn't have come on his own, but it was too late for regrets.

It was up to him to get Travis out of there. By any means possible.

Peeking around the corner, he caught a glimpse of Travis sitting in a hard-backed metal chair with his hands tied behind his back. Three young men, all about the same age as Miles Wayland, were standing off to the side.

"I will," Travis said. "I promise I'll call Gabe and have him come out here with the USB drive."

"You shouldn't have stolen his phone, Lonny," the guy who appeared to be in charge said. "What's going to happen when Train here calls the police department where his brother works?"

Fighting between the men was a good sign. Gabe could see that they were tired and nervous. They hadn't been prepared for this, and it showed.

Unfortunately, two of the men had guns tucked into their waistbands.

"Shut up!" Lonny said angrily. "I'm the brains behind this scheme, you're the idiot who messed everything up."

"Hey, calm down, both of you." The guy who did not have a weapon seemed to inch closer to Travis. Maybe his job was to guard his brother. If the guy in charge was Turk, then it was King who had taken up a position closer to Travis. "We've already raked in several hundred thousand dollars. We can walk away, Turk. We can walk away and use the technology again at some other time."

"Are you crazy?" Lonny demanded. "They'll find and arrest us."

"Not if we escape to Mexico or the Caribbean," King said. "We can work from anywhere, remember?"

For a moment, it seemed as if Turk was seriously considering the possibility. Then the guy glanced at Travis, and in that moment, Gabe feared they'd shoot his brother and head out of there.

"Don't move! I have a gun trained on the three of you," he said loudly. "I also have the USB drive, so I'm here to offer an exchange. The drive for Travis."

As a unit, the three men whirled to face the opening. Their facial expressions would have been comical if not for Turk and Lonny drawing their guns.

"Throw down your weapons," Gabe said in a sharp tone. "Don't make me shoot. All I want is Travis. You can have the USB drive."

"If he had a gun, he'd have shot us by now," Lonny said with a sneer.

"I don't want anyone to get hurt," Gabe said, knowing he was losing the upper hand. "The place is surrounded. Are you willing to die here today?"

When the two armed lifted their weapons, he knew the gig was up. He hadn't expected them to fall for it; he wasn't any good at this sort of thing. He was the team tech expert, not a cop!

Yet he had little choice but to see this through. Pulling the USB drive from his pocket, he stepped into the opening and held it up in the air where they could easily see it.

"I have the drive!" He did his best to look intimidating. "Release Travis and no one will get hurt!"

He heard a loud thump from somewhere outside. The panicked expression on Travis's face made him feel guilty. His brother had clearly expected more. The guy closest to him leveled his gun at his chest and fired just as the front door to the warehouse burst open.

The force of the bullet was shockingly painful, knocking him backward off his feet and stealing his breath.

He hit the floor hard, his head bouncing off the concrete floor.

For the second time in his adult life, he sank into dark oblivion.

***

CASSIDY HAD BEEN SO angry with the way Gabe had taken off to find Travis on his own that she could barely speak. What was wrong with him? Did he have a death wish? Gabe didn't even have a weapon!

Thankfully, Rhy took charge and pulled the team together.

"Okay, we know his location," Rhy had said as they'd set out for the warehouse. He'd insisted they all headed out in full tactical gear. "We'll surround the warehouse and use Brock to negotiate Travis's release."

"Gabe is likely inside too," she said, trying not to sound hurt by the way Gabe had taken off without telling her. "We need to take every precaution to make sure Gabe and Travis are not caught in the crossfire."

"Of course," Rhy had agreed.

She'd nodded, remaining silent as they'd jumped into the three SUVs and quickly covered the distance to the warehouse location Gabe had left on his computer screen. Just seeing how he'd identified the possible hideout had been like a kick to the chest.

So much for his having faith in her and the rest of the team, she thought with a grimace. Yeah, he was suffering from amnesia, but she and the others had proved their willingness to help and support him over the past thirty-six hours.

Yet he'd still gone off on his own.

Rhy wasn't happy about the situation either, but their boss had maintained his cool, calm demeanor. When they'd reached the deserted stretch of highway where Gabe had left their rental, she'd caught a flash of concern in Rhy's gaze.

"We'll go the rest of the way on foot," Rhy said. "Jina, you cover the front door with your long gun, and, Steele, you'll do the same at the back. Brock, you're our negotiator if needed. Flynn, you and Cassidy will breach from the front. Grayson, you cover the south, Roscoe the north, Raelyn and Joe will take the back." He raked his gaze over the group. The only missing teammate was Zeke who was still recovering from his shoulder injury. "I'll coordinate. Any questions?"

No one opened their mouth to speak. Cassidy knew that the members of the team were anxious to get to work.

Especially her. She was glad Rhy had allowed her to be a part of the breach team. She'd feared he'd ask her to sit this one out.

It had taken several tense minutes for them to get into their respective places. They had their earpieces in place, their radio on a private channel to minimize outside noise. Joe was the first one to break radio silence.

"Rear door is unlocked," he said in a low voice. "Assume Gabe accessed the building from this entry point."

Cassidy's stomach twisted so tightly she had to swallow against the urge to throw up. Of course, Gabe had gone inside with nothing in hand for a weapon.

Although she had noticed the USB drive was missing from his desk. She could just imagine his harebrained plan of using it to free Travis.

"Roger that," Rhy said in an equally soft voice. "We know they are likely armed and dangerous."

She glanced at Flynn. Brock opened his mouth to speak but hesitated when she lifted her hand to stop him. "Wait! I hear voices," she whispered.

No one moved. Cassidy crept closer to the door, straining to listen. When she heard Gabe's raised shout, demanding they throw down their weapons, she wanted to yank her hair out of her head with her bare hands. What was he doing? This wasn't a video game!

Then he went on to say the place was surrounded.

That gave her pause. Did he know they were outside? She hadn't seen any cameras, but it was possible. Knowing Gabe, though, this was probably another bluff. Either way, their time was running out.

She tapped her earpiece. "Things are escalating. No time. We'll need to breach the front and rear entrances before they realize Gabe is not armed," she whispered.

"Your call, Cass," Rhy said.

The responsibility was heavy, but she didn't hesitate. "On my count. Three, two, one." Flynn and Brock used the ram to break through the front door at the exact same time she heard Joe and Raelyn doing the same from the rear. Conscious of the fact that Jina and Steele were both using sniper rifles, she kept her head down as she ran through the front door.

The sound of gunfire kicked her pulse into high gear. "Police! Drop your weapons!"

In a flash, she saw the three men, two with guns. Travis was lying on the ground, cuffed to a chair that lay sideways beside him.

She grabbed the closest armed man, twisted the gun

from his hand, then pushed him toward the wall. Flynn was doing the same with the other.

The third man stood with his hands held high over his head. "I'm not armed! I'm with the FBI, and I'm not armed!"

The FBI? That was news to her, but she didn't take the time to consider the implications of an undercover cop. She quickly cuffed the man she had pressed against the wall, then turned to scan the room for Gabe.

"Man down," Joe said through the radio.

Gabe! She ran toward the sound of Joe's voice, nearly tripping over Gabe's prone figure sprawled on the ground in the opening between the front and back portions of the warehouse. He didn't move, his eyes closed, and for a moment, she feared he wasn't breathing.

"Gabe! Can you hear me?" She dropped to her knees beside him, running her fingers over his torso. It took her a second to realize he was still wearing the vest. Yanking the zipper of his coat down, she felt for the slug.

It was embedded in the Kevlar directly over his sternum. "Gabe, please open your eyes," she begged, as she moved her fingers over the vest. She didn't feel any blood, but she knew he was likely bleeding internally. "Call the Lifeline helicopter! Hurry!"

"On it," Rhy replied.

"He has a pulse," Joe said, his fingers palpating Gabe's carotid artery.

Tears blurred her vision, but she ruthlessly blinked them back. "Open your eyes, Gabe. It's over. Travis is safe."

Hearing his name, the seventeen-year-old came over to crouch beside them. Flynn or one of the others must have freed him from the chair. Travis looked gaunt and concerned. "Will he be okay? Turk shot him!"

Gabe let out a groan and lifted a hand to his chest. He cracked open an eyelid and peered at her. A smile tugged at the corner of his mouth. "Angel," he whispered. "My angel."

Was he delirious? She tried not to show her alarm when his hand dropped limply back to the ground as he closed his eyes. "Come on, Gabe. Stay with me. The Lifeline chopper will be here soon. You'll be taken to Trinity Medical Center where you'll get the best trauma care available. The danger is over. You're safe and so is Travis."

Gabe opened one eye, then the other. After focusing on her face for a moment, he said, "Wow. That hurt."

"Yeah, it hurts to get shot." She wanted to roll her eyes as much as she wanted to kiss him. Somehow, she refrained.

"I can't believe you came to find me," Travis said, addressing his brother. "And that you were going to trade the malware for my life!"

"Always," Gabe said. He grimaced, and then added weakly, "Least I could do since it was my fault you were involved."

She frowned. "You remember how this started? You remember getting the malware from Travis?"

Gaze shifted his gaze from Travis to her. Joe kept a hand on Gabe's wrist monitoring his pulse. "Yes. I remembered everything when I saw the warehouse. Listening in on the interview with Wayland helped, but for some reason seeing the warehouse on the map triggered my memory."

It was on the tip of her tongue to ask why he'd left without saying anything, but Rhy came over and squatted beside them. "Lifeline is on the way. They're going to land in the open field where we left our rides along with the rental. I sent Jina, Brock, and Steele to move the vehicles to give them room to land."

"Key to rental is in my pocket," Gabe said.

She dug it out, then tossed it to Rhy. Grabbing it midair, Rhy rose and headed out to join the others.

"Hey, take these cuffs off me!" one of the three men protested. "I told you I'm undercover with the FBI!"

"Maybe you are, maybe you aren't," Roscoe drawled in his Texas accent. "Won't believe it until I see some proof and know for sure you'all are one of the good guys. Until then, consider yourself under arrest. And if you are a fed, then I'm sure you understand you have the right to remain silent. That anything you say can and will be used against you in a court of law." Roscoe didn't stop until he'd recited the entire Miranda warning.

The guy sputtered, then gave up as he seemed to realize there was no point in fighting. Roscoe gave him a gentle shove, forcing him outside to wait for backup, sitting on the ground alongside the other two perps.

Everyone on the team knew Roscoe had trust issues when it came to those working for the federal government. She had no problem with his request to have proof before releasing the cuffs. She'd do the same thing, and she hadn't been betrayed by someone who was supposed to uphold the law.

Glancing at Travis, she asked, "What do you think? Did he give you any indication that he was with the FBI?"

Travis shrugged. "No, he didn't say anything like that. But King was the most decent guy in the group, more so even than Millions who took off the night we were at the Homerun restaurant."

"So you were there," she said.

"Yep. I called Gabe. You must be the one who answered." Travis sighed. "That was when things really took a turn for the worse. Turk caught me with the phone and threw a fit. King tried to keep Turk and Lonny calm, which didn't really work. They were both wound pretty tight at the way things were spiraling out of control. Especially after they realized Millions wasn't sticking with us."

"I'm sorry you had to go through that," she said, meaning it. Travis was much nicer than the mother he shared with Gabe. Must be the influence of their respective fathers.

Travis surprised her by giving her a hug. "Thanks for rescuing us."

"Ah, sure, anytime." She patted his back as Gabe beamed up at her with a goofy expression on his face. If she didn't know better, she'd think he'd been slipped some sort of pain medication or maybe laughing gas.

No way did a normal person grin like a loon after being shot, even while wearing a vest. She'd heard from those who were injured in the line of duty that it still hurt like the devil.

"I hear the chopper," Raelyn called.

Relief hit hard. Gabe was awake and talking. Hopefully, any internal bleeding he was experiencing wasn't too bad and could be easily fixed.

"I love you," Gabe said as the paramedics ran into the building, wheeling a gurney between them.

She was sure he didn't mean it, especially since he still wore that goofy grin. The one that made her wonder if he'd popped some pain pills while they weren't looking. Stepping back, she gave the paramedics room to work.

But Gabe's words echoed in her mind long after they were wheeling him back out to the waiting chopper.

"I love you too," she whispered, wishing she could fly back to Milwaukee with him in the chopper. Not possible since the Lifeline helicopter had a weight limit. And she and the rest of the team had a crime scene to process.

Soon, she silently promised. She'd be there soon. And if she had her way, she wouldn't leave until he was able to walk out of there on his own two feet.

CHAPTER FIFTEEN

Despite the medical staff surrounding him in the emergency department, Gabe's heart was full. He felt at peace knowing he'd told Cassidy how much he loved her.

He'd been poked, prodded, and taken for scans. He'd lost track of the time; he may have been there for one hour or twelve. The bright lights overhead hurt his head, so he closed his eyes and pictured Cassidy's concerned features. Just imagining her beautiful face helped him to relax. He didn't like knowing she was likely upset with him for leaving without her, but she and the rest of the team had come through for him. And for Travis.

He'd saved his younger brother. And that was all that mattered.

Feeling the sharp poke of a needle made him frown. It wasn't nearly as painful as the ache in his head and the pain spreading across his chest with every breath, but still. Wasn't he on the precipice of being welcomed into heaven by Jesus?

"Can you open your eyes?" a voice asked.

He did so, squinting against the light. A pretty face loomed over him, and he thought she looked familiar.

"I'm Dr. Finnegan, and you're at Trinity Medical Center," she said. "Can you tell me your name?"

That's right, she was Colin Finnegan's wife. Rhy's sister-in-law. Faye? Yes, Faye Finnegan. He remembered thinking that his boss was related to half the first responders in the city. "Gabe Melrose."

Dr. Finnegan nodded. "Great. And how are you feeling?"

That was an odd question to ask someone who was dying. "Like I was hit in the chest with a bullet."

"Yes, and you have quite the bruise to show for it. We're monitoring your heart closely to make sure you don't suffer an acute myocardial injury. You've had some irregular heartbeats, but nothing that requires additional treatment at this time."

What was she saying? His heart was bruised, but he wasn't dying? "I don't understand. I thought . . ." He let his voice trail off.

Faye rested a hand on his arm. "You're going to be fine, Gabe. We have done CT scans of your head and your chest. There's no internal bleeding, which is a relief, as we heard you have had two head injuries recently." She arched a brow as if he'd done it on purpose.

"Yeah. My head still hurts," he admitted. "So does my chest."

"I'm sure they do," Faye said with a nod. "We have the cardiology team involved in your care. They'll keep an eye on your heart for the next twenty-four hours, but if things continue to look good, you'll be discharged home to rest." Her expression turned stern. "And I mean rest. Not work. I know you're the technical backbone for Rhy's team, but you'll need to take it easy for a while."

"Okay." Discharged. He was shocked to hear that he'd be home soon. "Thank you."

"You're welcome." Faye's smile was kind. She had red hair, too, but wasn't nearly as beautiful as Cassidy.

He winced and shifted on the cot, realizing he'd told Cassidy he loved her because he thought he was dying. Now he wasn't, and he felt ridiculous for blurting out the truth like that.

Yet he couldn't regret his actions. Maybe she'd chalk it up to his being shot. He knew Cassidy only viewed him as a friend.

Although, hadn't she kissed him?

"Gabe?" Another beautiful face loomed over him, and this time he recognized Rhy's sister Alanna Carmichael. At least his memory was back, which was a minor miracle in itself. "We're going to move you to a private room, okay?"

"Yeah. Sure." He was in no position to argue, and a moment later, he found himself being wheeled through the hallway.

They hadn't gotten far when Cassidy rushed forward, grabbing the cart's side rails. "Gabe! You're okay?"

He couldn't help smiling up at her. She was so beautiful his heart ached. Not with pain, but in a good way. "I'm fine. Going home soon."

"Home!" Cassidy looked shocked.

"Maybe tomorrow," Alanna said. "His condition is stable, but the cardiology team is going to watch him closely to make sure his heart doesn't do anything funny. Surprisingly, though, he seems to have tolerated being shot in the chest fairly well."

"Have you given him pain medication?" Cassidy asked.

He lifted a hand to the bruise on his chest. "Don't need it."

"No, we have given him some fluids but nothing for pain. We can't risk masking a change in his condition related to his head injury," Alanna explained.

"You're sure he hasn't been given anything for pain?" Cassidy persisted. Her expression was concerned, and he wasn't sure why.

"I'm fine," he said. "Really."

Alanna nodded. "I'm sure. Would you like to walk with us to the cardiology unit?"

"I—yes. Thanks." Cassidy stepped to the side, and Alanna resumed pulling the foot of the cart. He had no idea who was pushing on the other end behind him. Cassidy reached over and took his hand. "We have the three men in custody, but we don't know who actually created the malware."

He thought briefly about Faye's directive to rest but thrust that aside. If the guy who'd orchestrated this mess was still out there, they needed to find him.

And soon.

"I need a laptop from the precinct," he said, even though he wasn't entirely sure how he'd find the mastermind of this thing.

"You're supposed to rest," Alanna said with a frown.

"Can't rest until we get this guy," Gabe said with a shrug. "I'll be more stressed if I don't do my part on this."

Alanna sighed and shook her head. "I'll leave that up to you and Rhy to work out."

Cassidy's expression was concerned. "Rhy will want you to rest."

He didn't say anything until he was settled in his new hospital room. The floor nurse chatted with Alanna, then came in to introduce herself. "My name is Diane. I'll be your nurse for the day."

Cassidy stood off to the side as Diane performed a quick exam. She glanced up at the heart monitor above his bed and nodded. "Everything looks good."

"Thanks." Once she was gone, he locked eyes with Cassidy. "I need a laptop."

She sighed. "I'll talk to Rhy. Even though he's not happy about how you took off on your own to go to the warehouse." She glanced away, staring at the wall. "I was hurt by that too."

"I'm sorry. I never wanted to hurt you or make Rhy angry. It's just—try to understand. I had to do everything possible to save Travis."

She finally turned to face him. "You almost died today, Gabe. That's not something to take lightly."

"I know. And I'm sorry about that." He grimaced. "I honestly didn't expect Turk to shoot me. I figured I'd stall long enough for you and Rhy and the others to arrive." And his plan had worked.

For the most part.

She bit her lip, then looked away again. He wished he wasn't in a hospital bed so he could pull her into his arms.

"I had faith in you, Cass. And in God. We're here today because of His grace." It was important to him that she realized he'd embraced the Lord.

Her phone rang. She pulled the device from her pocket. "Excuse me, I need to take this," she said. "This is my stepbrother Ben. I called him and Brian to warn them about the game."

As she moved toward the door, he heard her say, "Hey, Ben. I'm glad you called me back."

He remembered Cassidy telling him that her mother's new husband's sons were big gamers. And he'd found them on the Dorian site. He wondered how many gamers had already had their networks breached by playing the Sorcerer's Sword game. Die-hard fans wouldn't wait until Christmas to get it; they'd camp outside the store the minute the game went on sale.

Once he would have been among them, but his role within the Milwaukee Police Department had changed his priorities. He was more interested in supporting the team than in playing games.

If Travis hadn't reached out to him about discovering the malware embedded within the Sorcerer's Sword, he probably wouldn't be lying here connected to a heart monitor.

Cassidy was gone for so long he'd assumed she'd left without telling him. He stared up at the ceiling, praying she'd find it in her heart to forgive him.

Rhy too. And the rest of the team. Maybe he'd acted rashly, but given the same set of circumstances, he knew he'd make the same decision again.

But what he regretted the most was disappointing Cassidy. He loved her more than anything. It hurt to know that she didn't feel the same way.

And likely never would.

CASSIDY THOUGHT her conversation with Ben was odd. He had more questions about what had happened with

Gabe than the malware on the game. She'd had to cut it short to take a call from Rhy.

"Gabe wants a laptop, but the doctor has given him strict orders to rest," she said. "I'm torn because he's probably the best person to track this guy using the dark web. And Gabe claims he won't be able to rest until we know the truth."

"I'm torn too," Rhy agreed. "I've asked Brady to see if Ian can dig into the origin of the malware. But I'd feel better if Gabe were involved. Maybe I'm biased, but Gabe has been a great resource for us, and I believe in him. Besides, two brains working this are better than one."

"Do you want me to run back to the precinct?" she asked.

"No, I'll bring it. I need to talk to Gabe anyway," Rhy said. "I'm glad he's fine, but if he pulls another stunt like that, leaving without telling us, he'll be sorry."

She noticed he didn't threaten to fire Gabe, that would be like cutting off his nose to spite his face. "This was personal for him. And you know as well as I do, Rhy, most of the team members has put themselves in harm's way for their loved ones. Even you."

"Yeah, yeah. I know." Rhy sounded tired. "I'll see you soon." He ended the call without saying anything more.

She stood in the hallway for several minutes, wrestling with putting her conflicted feelings aside. She had been so angry with Gabe for leaving, then horrified and worried when he'd been shot.

He said he loved her, but she still didn't believe he was of sound mind. Maybe it was the shock of being hit at close range in the chest. Because if Gabe really did love her, why had he left without her?

From the moment he'd contacted her from the gas station, they'd been a team. Working together, side by side.

"I demand to speak to Gabe Melrose," a shrill voice said. She turned in time to see a woman standing in the hallway tapping her foot on the linoleum floor.

It didn't take long to recognize Gabe's mother.

Cassidy saw red and stalked toward her. "Ms. McCord? I'm police officer Cassidy Sommer. I'm afraid Gabe can't have visitors right now."

The woman's eyes narrowed, but Cassidy did not back down. Instead, she took a step forward, holding the older woman's gaze.

"Your son Travis is fine. Gabe was shot in the chest while wearing a Kevlar vest trying to protect him. But I will not tolerate anyone going into his room to upset him. So you can turn right back around and leave."

"I—really? He saved Travis?" Shelia McCord asked, her expression uncertain.

"Yes, he put his own life on the line for his *brother*." She stressed the last word. "And it would be wise of you to remember you have two sons. Not one, but two!"

Her words must have struck home because Shelia nodded. "You're right. I—thank you for telling me."

Cass was about to give in and let Gabe's mother visit when she turned and walked away. After watching her go, Cass turned and went back into Gabe's room.

He'd been resting, but his eyes shot open when he heard her come in.

"I thought you left," he said, his expression troubled. "I know you're upset with me. I'm so sorry. What can I do to make things better?"

"I'm fine." She forced a smile and crossed over to take his hand. "Your mom stopped by and is grateful for your help. I think she's feeling bad for the way she treated you. Oh, and Rhy's bringing a laptop . . ."

The door opened, and she turned, expecting to see Gabe's nurse.

But it was her stepbrother Ben who stood there with a hard expression on his face.

"You just couldn't stay out of it," he said, coming farther into the room. When he pulled a small gun from his coat pocket, she abruptly realized what had been so strange about their conversation.

Ben had known Gabe was injured and in the hospital. But she hadn't told him that. Now that he stood there, glaring at them, she realized Ben was involved.

As much if not more so than Turk and Lonny.

"You did this?" She wished she'd brought her service gun along, but she'd left it in the SUV's glove box. The hospital had a very clear no weapons rule, and she hadn't expected to need it.

"Stop right there," she said in her best cop voice. "You don't want to make this worse than it already is. Put the gun away and we'll talk. If you cooperate, I'll convince the DA's office to waive any jail time."

"Yeah, right," Ben sneered. "Your pal here is already onto us. And there's only one way to fix that." Ben abruptly reached over to grab one of Gabe's pillows and pressed it over the barrel of the gun. "Cheap silencer," he said with an eerie grin as he aimed the weapon toward Gabe.

Gabe yanked on the wires connected to electrodes on his chest and rolled to the side, causing the monitor to alarm loudly at the same time she launched herself at Ben. The gun went off, sending her heart into her throat. She slammed Ben against the bathroom door, fighting to rip the gun from his hands.

Anger and fear gave her the strength of ten men. Every minute she'd worked out with Jina and Raelyn at the MMA gym had paid off. She wrenched the gun free while planting her elbow sharply into Ben's ribs. He howled in pain, but she didn't stop there. She brought her knee up into his groin and then brought the butt of his gun down hard on the back of his head.

Gabe was out of bed, his gaze frantic as they towered over Ben who was curled in a ball on the floor. "Are you okay?"

"Peachy," she said breathlessly, looking for something to use to tie Ben's wrists together. Spying one of the heart monitor wires lying on the bed, she grabbed it and used it as a binding to secure Ben. "You?"

"You better teach me how to shoot," Gabe said with a sigh. Then he gestured toward the heart monitor. "Oh, he shot and killed that thing." She hadn't noticed the alarm in the room had fallen silent.

But the initial alarm had done the trick. Several staff members ran into the room, looking on with astonishment at how Cassidy finished tying Ben's wrists behind his back.

"Sorry about the damage," Cassidy said, feeling guilty over the destroyed hospital equipment. "He got a shot off before I was able to take him down."

"I'm calling security," one of the nurses said, stepping back outside the room.

She reached down and dragged her bound stepbrother to his feet. "You're under arrest for attempted murder," she said, then proceeded to read him his rights. Gabe weakly sat back down on the edge of the bed, looking grim.

When she finished, he asked, "Is your stepbrother's username Axe? I know I found them both under their own names, but I'm sure he created a new identity to help hide his actions."

She had no idea, but the flash of guilt over Ben's features confirmed Gabe's suspicions.

"I saw his screen name linked with the Turk and commenting on Travis's post downplaying the danger," Gabe said. "Now we know Axe is Ben. I'm sure we'll find everyone else involved, in this too."

She nodded trying to hide her guilt. Logically, she knew she was not responsible for her stepbrother's actions.

Five minutes later, the room was full of people. Rhy had arrived with the laptop, and the security guards had called the local police, who had hauled Ben away. Gabe's mother, Shelia, had returned to the room to see her son, and Cassidy was glad when Shelia actually hugged and thanked Gabe for what he did for Travis, before being hustled away by the security team.

They spent nearly an hour giving their statements and explaining what had transpired. At some point during the process, Rhy spoke at length to Ian and filled Cassidy in on the latest aspect of the case. Then Rhy finally convinced the authorities to let her and Gabe go, promising to work together to close this incident.

The hospital staff moved Gabe to another room, but he stood with his arms crossed over his chest, threatening to leave against medical advice. "I'll sign whatever you bring me, but I'm not staying."

The nurse sent Cass a harried look.

She took a deep breath and let it out slowly. "Come on, Gabe, work with me," she pleaded. "Ben is under arrest, and Rhy has tasked the rest of the team with finding and arresting Brian. Ian was able to pick up the investigation where you left off and has implicated both of my stepbrothers in this." She frowned, then added, "Apparently, my stepbrothers were smart enough to not only make the malware, but to hack the game's operating system to insert it." She still couldn't believe they were involved. Ben had once told her they were given beta versions of games to test them out. She doubted the company had expected anyone to use the beta version of a game for something like this. "According to Ian, they probably worked on it for six months straight, planning to reap in the bulk of their cash over the Christmas holiday once the game had been uploaded to millions of homes across the United States and even worldwide."

"Until Travis noticed and raised the alarm," Gabe said, finally sinking down onto the edge of the bed. "He's a brilliant kid with a bright future."

"He is," she agreed with a smile. "He takes after you, Gabe. Travis is the kind to use his talent for good, not evil." Unlike her stepbrothers, she thought grimly.

"So that's it?" Gabe asked uncertainly. "It's really over?"

"Yes." She fought a wave of exhaustion brought on by the second adrenaline crash of the day. And she was secretly relieved she didn't have to kill Ben, the way she had shot Taylor's cousin last month. She managed a smile. "Please stay. I won't be able to relax until I know your heart hasn't been damaged by all of this."

"Yeah, okay." He stretched out on the bed. The way he absently rubbed the center of his chest made her realize he was still hurting.

"Thank you." She dropped into the chair next to his bed.

He was silent for a long minute. "Cass?" He spoke in a low, hesitant voice. "Do you think you can find a way to forgive me?"

"Forgive you?" At first she didn't understand, then she realized he had picked up the thread of their conversation before Ben had rudely interrupted to threaten them with a gun. She leaned forward to take his hand. "Of course, I forgive you," she said. "I was a little hurt that you didn't include me in your plan after we'd been working so well as a team, but your health is all that matters."

His expression betrayed his relief. "I'm glad. Because I love you so much."

Love? He'd said those words to her back in the warehouse, but he'd been delirious at the time.

Hadn't he?

"It's okay. I know you don't feel the same way," he said quickly. "I wanted you to know how I felt in case I didn't make it."

"Oh, Gabe." She slowly stood, searching his gaze. "I care about you, too, but I seem to remember you saying once that you didn't think you could handle being with a cop. And since that's exactly why Wade left me, I figured anything more between us was out of the question."

"I don't remember saying that," he protested. "And if I did, I only meant that I hated knowing you were in danger, Cass. Not because I can't handle it. But because I love you."

She frowned. "Okay, I know you're saying that now, but being in danger has a way of magnifying feelings to unrealistic proportions."

He quirked a brow. "Fancy talk for someone who's clueless," he said. "It's your turn to listen to me, Cass. When I couldn't remember my own name, I remembered yours. When I didn't know my own address, I was able to give the gas station guy your phone number. I've loved you for months, Cass. My feelings have nothing to do with the way we've faced danger over the past two days. I fell in love with you long before this."

"He's right," Steele drawled, coming into the room. The rest of the team quickly gathered around them, each of them grinning like maniacs. She was starting to wonder if they'd all lost their minds when Jina shot her an exasperated look.

"Cass, Gabe's feelings for you have been obvious to everyone," she said. "What we all want to know is how you feel about him."

"Yeah, fess up," Roscoe drawled.

"Come on, Cass, tell us you're not as clueless as Gabe accused you of being," Brock said.

Grayson, Flynn, and Raelyn simply stared at her.

She turned back to face Gabe. "I love you. More than I've ever thought possible."

"Woot!" Flynn shouted. "It's time for another wedding!"

"Yours first," Raelyn said, giving him an elbow to the ribs. "Then Cassidy and Gabe's."

"I'd like to ask all of you to leave," Gabe said, his gaze never leaving hers. "We don't need an audience for this."

To her surprise, the team turned and left the room. Gabe slid off the bed and took both of her hands in his.

"This is just between you and me, Cassidy," he said somberly. "I don't want you to feel pressured by the others. Take some time, maybe we can, you know, go out on a couple of dates." He said the words casually, but the tips of his ears burned red.

And that's when she realized he always blushed like that when they were alone together. The rest of the team was right. She had been clueless. She'd let her personal experience with Wade blind her feelings.

But not anymore.

"I don't need time, Gabe. I love you. When you were shot . . ." She shook her head helplessly. "I thought I'd lost you forever."

He drew her close and kissed her. She wrapped her arms around his neck, pulling him close as she kissed him back.

"They're kissing," she heard Grayson say. "I think that seals the deal."

"It's about time," Brock muttered.

"I'll call Zeke," Flynn offered. "He'll want to hear the news."

Gabe broke off from their kiss, breathing hard. "Bunch of idiots," he muttered. But then a slow grin spread across his features, and he began to laugh. "We work with a bunch of idiots!" Cassidy couldn't help but laugh too.

"You may as well all come back inside," Gabe said between chuckles.

Their teammates hadn't gone far, and it made Cassidy laugh that much harder at the thought of the seven of them huddling outside Gabe's room listening in.

Bunch of morons for sure, but they were her morons. Hers and Gabe's.

They rushed in, enveloping her and Gabe with unfettered exuberance.

Kissing hadn't made his monitor alarm, but it began to shrill now, once again bringing several staff members rushing into the room.

"Okay, that's it." The older nurse planted her hands on her ample hips. "Everyone out. Visiting hours are over."

"Cassidy stays," Gabe said, keeping his arm around her waist. He glanced at her, as if expecting she might disagree.

"Yes, I'm staying," she confirmed.

The rest of the group good naturedly took their leave. When they were alone again, she kissed Gabe. "I love you," she whispered.

"I love you too." He gave her that same goofy smile that made her think he was high on meds.

Maybe that was his *I'm in love* expression. He was so adorable the thought made her smile again.

Because she felt the same way. Loving Gabe made her feel as if nothing could go wrong. That their future would be bright with joy and happiness.

Like Christmas itself.

EPILOGUE

One week before Christmas . . .

Gabe helped Cass with the last of the decorations for the team Christmas party. Everyone on the team, their respective families, and even their kids were planning to attend.

There wasn't anything more to do on the case. He had tracked the computer virus that had sabotaged their precinct to Cassidy's stepbrother Brian. Rhy had confirmed the fingerprints at the scene of the Homerun restaurant had implicated Turk and Lonny, who along with Ben and Brian would spend a very long time in jail for their crimes.

His mother had shocked him by calling to apologize even after they'd briefly chatted in the hospital. He'd assured her everything was fine. He didn't anticipate having a close relationship with her, but at least it was no longer antagonistic.

And that was in the past. Today was a time for celebration. One he'd looked forward to.

Surprisingly, Zeke, Sienna, and Bailey were the first to arrive.

"Zeke!" Cassidy rushed over to give him a hug. "You look great! You too, Sienna," she said, embracing Zeke's wife.

"Up, up!" Bailey said. Gabe lifted the little girl into his arms, his heart melting when she patted his cheeks. "Abe. Abe."

"We've been teaching her your name," Zeke said with a grin. "She has trouble with some letters."

"You're a sweetie," he said, giving her a quick kiss on the top of her head. "I'll be your Uncle Abe, okay?"

"Abe!" Bailey repeated, then squirmed to get down. Bemused, he set her back on her feet. Just then Flynn and Taylor walked in. Instantly, Bailey ran toward them. "Flynn! Flynn!" she called.

"What am I, chopped liver?" Cassidy asked as Flynn lifted Bailey into his arms.

"She seems to prefer men these days," Sienna said with a sigh. "I'm sure that's Zeke's fault."

"Hey, I'm not any happier about that than you are," Zeke protested. "I'll have to sit on the porch with my service weapon when she starts dating."

More teammates arrived, and soon the hall was full to the brim. Rhy and his very pregnant wife, Devon, had brought their fourteen-month-old daughter, Colleen. Brock and his wife, Liana, looked happy, their marriage stronger now than ever before. Joe and his pregnant wife, Elly, stayed near Rhy and Devon. From the concern in Joe's eyes, Gabe could tell he was worried about Elly overdoing things as she was due on the day after Christmas. Steele and Harper brought their seven-month-old daughter, Amelia, and soon the three girls, Bailey, Amelia, and Colleen were playing together in a corner of the room.

Roscoe and Libby also had a baby boy named Freddy,

but the two-month-old was too young to play on the floor with the others. Raelyn and Isaiah brought their adopted son, Leon, too. At thirteen, he seemed more inclined to hang out near the adults than with the little kids. Last Gabe heard, Raelyn and Isaiah were also planning to expand their family, either by having a baby of their own or adopting another.

Maybe both.

Grayson and his wife, Eve, were also expecting. Jina and her husband, Cole, were allegedly heading down that same path as were Brock and Liana. As he gazed around the room, Gabe realized there would be no better time than this.

He loudly clapped his hands to get everyone's attention. It took a few minutes, but then Rhy whistled loudly through his teeth, and that was enough to make everyone stop talking.

"Ah, thanks, Rhy." Gabe tried not to look as nervous as he felt. "First, I'd like to thank you all for putting your lives on the line to rescue me." He knew his way of fighting crime, from behind a computer screen, was important, too, but not in the same way they put themselves in danger.

"Oh," Elly called out loudly. "Oh, no!"

"What?" Joe demanded. "Don't tell me . . ."

"Um, yes, I think I'm in labor." Elly put her hands over her belly. "The contractions are coming faster now."

"Faster?" Rhy and Joe echoed in horrified unison.

"Yes, sorry. I wasn't sure they were real," Elly said with a shrug. "I wanted to come to the party."

Gabe watched as several of the pregnant women gathered around Elly, helping her into her coat as Joe looked on, his eyes wide with terror, as if he might throw up.

"Get her to the hospital, Joe," Rhy said, clapping his brother-in-law on the back. "And keep us updated."

"Let's go, Elly." Joe pulled himself together, escorting his wife to the door. Then Joe glanced back and gave Gabe a knowing grin and nodded. As if he knew what Gabe had intended to do and was giving his approval.

"Sorry, go ahead, Gabe," Rhy said, getting everyone in the room back on track. "What were you saying?"

He reached over, took Cassidy's hand, then went down on one knee. He pulled the engagement ring box from his pocket and offered it to her. "Cassidy, will you please marry me?"

For a long second, the room was dead silent, everyone, even the kids, seemingly waiting for her answer.

"Oh, Gabe, yes!" Cassidy almost knocked the ring box from his fingers as she threw herself into his arms. "Yes, I'll marry you!"

The room erupted into applause and shouts of congratulations. Gabe didn't really bother to pay attention to their teammates. He was just thankful Cassidy had said yes.

"Merry Christmas, Cassidy," he whispered.

"Merry Christmas, Gabe," she whispered back. "I love you."

"I love you too."

"Here's to the soon-to-be Mr. and Mrs. Gabe Melrose," Zeke declared, lifting his glass of hot cider.

"Hear, hear!" the rest of the group chimed in.

"I can hardly wait," Cassidy said as he finally put the ring on her finger.

He couldn't wait to make her his wife either. He held her close, reveling in the warmth of her love, thrilled to have those closest to them, maybe not tied together by DNA, but family all the same, here to celebrate with them.

. . .

I HOPE you enjoyed Gabe and Cassidy's story! This was such a fun series to write, and I'm blessed to have readers like you who stayed with me along the way.

I'm kicking off a new series next month, the Sullivan K9 Search and Rescue series. The first book will feature FBI Agent Doug Bridges (remember him?) as he heads out west to find his missing sister with the help of a very talented K9 search and rescue team. If you're interested in reading *Scent of Danger*, click here!

DEAR READER

Thanks so much for reading my Oath of Honor series. I'm truly blessed to have wonderful readers like you. I hope you enjoyed Gabe and Cassidy's story. It was fun bringing the entire team back together for one last mission.

I am excited about my new Sullivan K9 Search and Rescue series! If you enjoyed the Callahans and Finnegans, you'll love the Sullivans, a large family of dog lovers dedicated to finding those in danger and fighting crime. DEA Agent Doug Bridges will be the first to use their services as he desperately searches for his missing sister. I hope you'll give his story *Scent of Danger* a try!

Don't forget, you can purchase ebooks or audiobooks directly from my website will receive a 15% discount by using the code **LauraScott15**.

I adore hearing from my readers! I can be found through my website at https://www.laurascottbooks.com, via Facebook at https://www.facebook.com/LauraScott Books, Instagram at https://www.instagram.com/laurascott books/, and Twitter https://twitter.com/laurascottbooks. Please take a moment to subscribe to my YouTube channel at youtube.com/@LauraScottBooks-wr1xl?sub_confirmation=1. Also take a moment to sign up for my monthly newsletter to learn about my new book releases! All subscribers receive a free novella not available for purchase on any platform.

Until next time,

Laura Scott

PS: Read on for a sneak peek of *Scent of Danger*.

SCENT OF DANGER

Chapter One

His halfsister was late.

DEA Agent Doug Bridges nursed his coffee, trying to ignore the sliver of apprehension sliding down his spine as he stared out the window of the Hitching Post Café in Cody, Wyoming. Emily had recently moved to the area from Jackson and worked the night shift as a nurse in the emergency department, so there was no reason to panic. One of her patients could have crashed in the middle of shift change.

Yet it was nearly forty-five minutes since their designated meeting time. The interior of the café was warm, especially compared to the outside temperature of a whopping 12 degrees. He was glad the snow had stopped after blanketing the town with two inches of fluff the night before. Now the sun was trying to peek out from behind the clouds that hung over the Bighorn Mountains.

For what seemed like the hundredth time, he glanced at his silent phone, willing it to ring. It didn't. He finally picked it up and called Emily, hoping she'd say she was on her way.

Straight to voice mail.

The niggling concern grew. He finished his coffee and pulled some cash from his pocket to cover the tab. Sitting in the café wasn't helping. He was supposed to head to the Yellowstone Regional Airport to catch his flight that would take him through Denver, then home to Milwaukee, Wisconsin. Emily wouldn't miss their last meal together without a good reason.

Doug shrugged into his thick winter coat and drew on a woolen hat and gloves. He hadn't expected Wyoming to be that much colder than Wisconsin, but he'd underestimated the impact of the mountains and the wind.

He left the Hitching Post and slid in behind the wheel of his four-wheel-drive rental SUV. He'd head over to the hospital to meet Emily. If there was time, they could grab a bite in the cafeteria. He didn't want to leave without saying goodbye. Having worked with the Finnegans and the Callahans over the past few years, he'd decided to mend his relationship with his family.

Hence spending the Christmas and New Year holidays with his halfsister, Emily.

The drive to the local medical center didn't take long. The hospital was located on the far west side of town, and they'd purposefully chosen the Hitching Post as a meeting spot because it was halfway between the medical facility and his hotel.

The parking lot was only half full, and when he saw Emily's Jeep covered in a two-inch layer of snow, he relaxed. Good to know she was still working. He pulled into the open space next to hers and shut down the engine. Hunching his shoulders against the chill, he stood for a moment, glancing around the area, then strode inside the emergency department entrance.

The waiting room was empty except for two people who were hacking up half a lung. Feeling bad for them, he went to the front desk. A plump woman who was old enough to be his grandmother glanced up at him expectantly. Her name tag identified her as Barbara. "May I help you?"

He smiled. "Hi, I'm Emily's brother, Doug Bridges. Can you let her know I'm waiting for her?"

Barbara frowned. "Emily left almost an hour ago."

The niggling concern billowed into full-fledged alarm. "What do you mean? Her car is still out in the parking lot."

"It is?" Barbara appeared flustered. "I don't understand. Emily waved at me as she left, explaining how she was meeting her brother for breakfast at the Post. I don't think she'd walk to the café in this weather."

No, she wouldn't. Doug instantly went into federal agent mode. "I want to talk to someone in charge, and I need to see your video camera footage."

Barbara's eyes widened, and she reached for the phone. "Stan? You better get out here. Seems as if Emily might be missing."

Stan strode toward him a long minute later. He was in his mid-fifties and was wearing what appeared to be a security officer uniform. "I'm Stan Turner, the security officer for the hospital. You're Emily's brother?"

"Yes, Doug Bridges." He shook Stan's hand, briefly wondering if the entire hospital staff knew his sister. "I need to see your camera footage. Barbara saw Emily leave, but her car is still outside in the parking lot. And she didn't meet me for breakfast as planned."

Stan hesitated for a moment, as if deciding if he should comply, then nodded. "Okay. Follow me."

His small office was located just beyond the waiting area. It took the older man so long to pull up the video it was all Doug could do not to thrust him aside to figure it out for himself.

"Emily's shift would have ended at seven thirty," Stan said. He poked at the keyboard, then used the mouse. "Here she is."

Doug wedged himself behind the desk so he could see the computer screen. His gut tightened when he saw Emily waving at Barbara, seemingly saying something as she headed toward the main entrance. His sister was wearing her cherry-red parka coat, her blond hair covered by a matching red hat and gloves. Within seconds, she went through the automatic doors and disappeared around the corner, seemingly toward the parking lot.

"Okay, can you switch to one of the outside cameras?" Doug asked. "You must have one that overlooks the parking lot."

"We do," Stan agreed. He pulled up two more cameras before finding the right one. He fast-forwarded to match the time frame of the previous camera. Then he hit the play button.

There was nothing. No sign of Emily crossing the parking lot to her car.

"Back it up," Doug said feeling grim. "Maybe the clocks between the cameras don't match."

"They match," Stan protested. "They're on the same system." But he did as Doug asked, backing up the video for a full five minutes earlier. The silence hung heavy as they watched as nobody walked past for a full fifteen minutes.

That's when a car pulled into the lot, and one of the coughing patients got out and came inside.

That was it. No sign of Emily. Or anyone else, which he found odd. He frowned, staring at Stan. "Okay, pull up the cameras facing the other way. Maybe she saw someone she knew and went over to speak with them."

Stan flushed. "We don't have cameras overlooking the street. We only have them covering the main entrance, the emergency department entrance, and the parking lot."

Three cameras? Really? "Okay, bring up the main entrance." He tried not to show his frustration. Milwaukee wasn't anywhere near as large as Chicago, Detroit, or Minneapolis, but he happened to know that Trinity Medical Center had over six hundred cameras covering the property. Three seemed ridiculous.

More seconds dragged by as Stan manipulated the screen. "Here we are," he finally said.

Several people could be seen using the main entrance, despite the early hour. But none of them were Emily.

"Maybe you oughta call the police," Stan said, his expression mirroring Doug's concerns. "Seems strange that Emily would vanish like that."

"Thanks. Would you please send me a copy of that emergency department video?" He hoped the security guard would cooperate, but if he didn't, Doug had no trouble using his badge to go over his head. "Please," he added. "That's Emily's last-known location. Proof that she left, at least originally, under her own power."

"Okay, where should I send it?" Stan asked.

Doug quickly provided his email address, waiting until the message had popped up on his phone before stepping back. "Thank you."

"Anytime," Stan said. "You know, before you head to

the police department, you should make sure Emily didn't head home. Maybe she caught a ride with someone because she was having car trouble."

He nodded without pointing out that didn't make sense. The camera would have shown Emily walking to her car, trying to start it, then coming back inside. She'd call him or walk to the café to meet him. It was as if she'd stepped into an alternate universe, if you believed in that sort of thing.

He didn't. His earlier apprehension returned in full force. He walked back through the emergency department, trying not to think about how long Emily had been gone. A full hour by now, maybe a little more.

He hated knowing the trail had already grown cold. Literally and figuratively.

Outside the emergency department, he paused to glance around. As before, he didn't see anything suspicious. Both corners of the building were out of camera range, so he turned toward the side of the building closest to the parking lot.

Forcing himself to stop and think, he took a moment to clear his mind. This was not the time to make a mistake. He stood back, slowly raking his gaze over the ground. His heart thumped when he noticed what appeared to be several footprints crisscrossing in the snow.

He scanned the length of the building, then looked up to locate the camera. When he found it, he grimly realized that anyone walking along the building itself would be able to stay out of sight.

A chill that had nothing to do with the freezing temperatures washed over him. Moving forward, he followed the side building until he reached the ambulance bay. Of course, there were no cameras overlooking that area.

He turned and retraced his steps, his thoughts whirling.

In his mind's eye, he could imagine someone standing near the corner, maybe showing distress as that person asked Emily for help.

And then what? Kidnapped her?

It was hard to imagine anyone doing that, but what was the alternative? Doug hurried back to his rental, mentally making a list of tasks. Check Emily's house. Go to the local police department. Call his boss, Special Agent in Charge Donovan, to explain he wouldn't be back to work as planned.

And from there? As a federal agent, he knew how to investigate crimes, specifically drug trafficking. But out here in the middle of small-town Wyoming, he was at a distinct disadvantage.

He'd need help from local experts. And soon.

Before Emily was hurt or killed.

MAYA SULLIVAN SLID out from behind the wheel of her specially designed K9 SUV and clicked the button to open the back. The door rose, but Zion, her Siberian Husky, didn't jump down.

"Come, Zion," she said sternly. "You like Dr. Andrew, remember?"

Her K9 partner still didn't move. Suppressing a sigh, she moved closer to look directly into the blue eyes of her partner. "Out!"

Zion jumped down as if she'd been waiting for the magic word. This was a routine vet visit for Zion, and usually the husky was anxious and raring to go.

As she closed the back hatch, a voice came from behind her. "Ms. Sullivan?"

She whirled, her hand going to the pocket of her coat that contained her gun. Recently she'd caught a glimpse of someone following her, and suddenly there was a tall stranger standing there. Zion came over to stand protectively in front of her.

Seeing the dog, the stranger abruptly stopped. "Are you Maya Sullivan?"

She tried to relax. As the oldest of nine siblings residing on the Sullivan K9 Search and Rescue ranch, she was often called upon by strangers. Although usually not while she was in town visiting the vet. "Yes, I'm Maya, and this is Zion, my K9 partner. May I ask who you are?"

"Doug Bridges." A look of relief flashed in his eyes. "I've heard great things about you and your ranch, and I'm in desperate need of your expertise."

Maya dropped her hand from her pocket and resisted the urge to glance at her watch. She forced a smile. "I'm sorry, but Zion has a nine-o'clock appointment inside. I'll be happy to chat with you when that's finished."

"No, I can't wait that long." Bridges took a step closer, causing Zion to growl low in her throat. He stopped where he was, his gaze beseeching. "Please. My sister, Emily Sanders, went missing at seven thirty-five this morning. She's a nurse and left the hospital after her night shift, then disappeared. I'm desperately in need of your search-and-rescue services."

"Emily? Emily Sanders is your sister?" She narrowed her gaze, eyeing him with suspicion. "Funny, the last time I saw Emily she didn't mention a brother."

"Halfbrother," he clarified. "I—we haven't really interacted with each other much until the past few months." A gust of cold wind hit hard, making her realize they were standing around in the freezing temperatures. "How do you know my sister?"

Maya wasn't in the mood to discuss how Emily had treated her youngest sister Kendra in the emergency department after a terrible fall. Her family's personal life was none of his concern. But knowing Emily was missing gave her pause. "Are you sure she's not at home? Or still working?"

His green eyes flared with anger, but he didn't yell or shout. "I'm sure. I've been to the hospital and have video of her leaving through the front entrance. But her car is still there covered in snow from last night, and she never crossed the parking lot. I double-checked her house and went to the local police." Now his mouth tightened. "I've filed a missing persons report, but the officer on duty basically told me I would be better off hiring someone from the Sullivan search-and-rescue ranch than waiting for them to find her. I was about to head that way when I saw your car."

She didn't bother to glance at the SUV with the Sullivan K9 Search and Rescue logo stenciled along the side. That had been her brother Chase's bright idea, and lately when she'd sensed someone following her, she'd been tempted to cover it with paint.

Another cold blast of air convinced her that standing out here talking wasn't smart. She couldn't walk away from this. Missing persons cases happened to be Zion's specialty. With a sigh, she nodded. "I'll help search for Emily. First, I need you to step closer."

His expression uncertain, he did as she asked. She put a hand on his arm. "Friend, Zion. Doug is a friend."

Zion sniffed his feet, then wagged her tail. Doug gave her a grateful look.

"Okay, now that Zion knows you're not the enemy, let's get back inside the SUV where it's warmer."

Doug didn't hesitate to open the passenger door. She clicked the fob to open the back and gave Zion the hand gesture to get inside. Zion tilted her head—as if to ask, *Are you sure?*—before jumping inside.

Sliding in behind the wheel, she started the engine, then used her phone to call the vet. Easier to call to say she was out on a search than to do that in person. Thankfully, Dr. Andrew didn't mind her frequent need to reschedule. As she slid the gear shift into drive, she glanced at Doug. "You're not from this area, are you?"

He looked surprised. "No, why, is it that obvious?"

She smiled. "You speak with a distinct Midwest accent."

"Milwaukee, Wisconsin," he said. "I can pay via credit card, a check, or cash. Whatever works for you."

She waved that off and turned to drive back to the hospital. Zion didn't stretch out to rest but kept her nose pressed to the crate as if intending to keep Doug Bridges in line. "Don't worry about payment. As far as searching for your sister, it's best if you have a scent source for her. Some sort of clothing. If that's not possible, Zion may be able to pick up her scent regardless, especially if I give her a few locations to work from. Can you tell me a little about Emily's personal life? Is she seeing someone?"

Doug seemed relieved to see the hospital looming on the horizon. He drew a pair of black gloves from his pocket. "These belong to Emily. I took them when I checked to make sure she hadn't gone home. To answer your question, Emily is not seeing anyone now that I'm aware of, but she did break up with her previous boyfriend roughly four months ago. That's one of the reasons she relocated from Jackson to Cody. She claimed Avery wasn't the least bit upset about the split as he was planning to move to Colorado anyway. I guess he's some sort of ski instructor."

"Ah yes, Avery White," she said with a nod. "I'm not surprised he plans to leave Wyoming for Colorado. He seemed to think he was destined for bigger things."

"Does everyone know everyone else in this town?" There was a sharp edge to his tone.

"For the most part, yes. But I've done some skiing in the Tetons; Avery acted like he owned the place." Maya shot him a quick glance before she pulled into the parking lot. "Which car is Emily's?"

"That burgundy Jeep."

Seeing the vehicle, she nodded, then parked two spaces away. Keeping the engine on, she pulled a plastic bag from the glove box and carefully dropped Emily's gloves inside. "I'd like you to stay back to give Zion some room to work."

"Ms. Sullivan," he began.

"Maya," she quickly interjected. "We don't use formal titles around here."

"Okay, then call me Doug. I'm a federal agent with the DEA, and I would like to give you my working theory before you put Zion to work."

She held up a hand to stop him. "Really, it's better if you don't. I'm sure you're an excellent agent, but I won't go into this with preconceived ideas. We need to let Zion do her thing and go from there, okay?"

He frowned but nodded. "Okay."

While she found his career interesting, she wasn't going to let that interfere with how she and Zion worked together as a team. She released the back hatch, and this time, Zion eagerly jumped down. Zion's thick white and gray coat kept her warm during winter searches, and she held her curvy tail high as she sniffed the air.

As was her habit, Maya placed the vest over Zion's head, a physical indication they were going to work. Then she filled a bowl with water and set it down on the ground. Water moistened the dog's mucus membranes, which enhanced her ability to follow scents. Zion only took two laps, then stared up at Maya with her pale blue eyes, waiting for her next command.

"Good girl," Maya praised, as she ran her fingers through Zion's thick gray and white coat. "Are you ready? Are you ready to work?" The dog was always raring to go, but she liked to amp up Zion's excitement. She took the plastic bag containing Emily's gloves from her pocket and opened it. "Emily," she said, giving the scent a name. She preferred using names on cases where they knew exactly who the victim was. "Search Emily."

Zion burned her snout deep into the bag for a long moment. Then she had her head up and was sniffing the air. Maya was far too aware of Doug standing beside the SUV, watching them.

After a few seconds of sniffing, Zion whirled in a circle and bounded toward the burgundy Jeep. The K9 sniffed the ground around the car, then sat at the driver's side door and turned to stare intently up at Maya.

"Good girl," she praised, pulling a stuffed yellow bunny from her pocket. She tossed it into the air, and Zion leaped up to grab it. Then she shook her head back and forth, running in a circle as if oblivious to the frigid temps. Huskies loved to goof around.

Maya half expected Doug to protest the play time, but he remained silent. Maybe his experience was such that he knew working dogs needed to be rewarded for a job well done. She waited for Zion to return to her side. "Hand," she said. With reluctance, Zion regurgitated the stuffed bunny into her gloved palm. "Good girl. Are you ready? Search! Search Emily."

Eager to get back to work, Zion sniffed the ground around the Jeep, then trotted toward the front entrance to the emergency department. Maya followed a few paces behind, not giving the dog any indication of where to go.

Zion sniffed around the doorway, then sat again, turning to look up at her. "Good girl," she praised, but kept the bunny in her pocket. "Search! Search for Emily."

Understanding her job wasn't done, Zion sniffed the ground again, then went to the corner of the building. It was the side of the building that faced the parking lot. Nose to the ground, Zion trotted along the side of the building until she reached the driveway leading to the ambulance bay. Then she sat again, staring up at Maya intently.

"Good girl," she repeated. "Search for Emily."

Zion seemed to shoot her an exasperated glance before she went back to work. The husky sniffed all around the ground but returned to the exact same spot she'd alerted on before. Maya's heart sank. This appeared to be the end of the trail.

"Good girl," she said with forced enthusiasm, and tossed the bunny into the air. As always, Zion caught it and trotted along holding the stuffed animal proudly, as if she'd won the biggest prize at the state fair.

"That's impressive," Doug said from behind her. She turned to glance at him. "Your K9 proved my theory. I think someone parked in the ambulance bay and convinced Emily to come down along the side of the building to help. Then they kidnapped her."

She didn't like hearing that. "No video for the ambulance area?"

"No." He glanced around the area. "Can your dog track people taken by car?"

"No. Sometimes in the summer if the windows are open, some dogs can catch the scent if it's a calm day, but those instances are rare. It would help if we knew the general direction they were headed. We could perform a search grid."

"I've been thinking about that," Doug said thoughtfully. "Maybe we should check the closest hotels in the area, see if your K9 can pick up Emily's scent."

She frowned. "I'm not sure going from one hotel to the next is a good use of time."

"I'm open to other ideas," Doug's jaw tightened with repressed anger. "But we don't have anything else to go on. I've tried calling Emily at least twelve times. The call goes straight to voice mail. Either the phone battery died or the device is powered down."

With a grimace, she shrugged. "Okay, we'll check the hotels. But understand this, I will need to give Zion plenty of rest breaks, especially if we're outside in the cold for any length of time."

He nodded. "Of course. I wouldn't want anything to happen to your dog. If you don't mind, we can start at my hotel, the Lumber Jack Inn. Emily was never there that I'm aware of. Besides, I need to let the front desk know that I'm staying longer than planned."

"That's fine." She focused on Zion. "Hand."

Zion trotted over and placed the stuffed bunny in her outstretched hand.

"She's really amazing," Doug said as they walked back to the SUV.

"Zion is one of our best search dogs," Maya admitted. Once they were settled in the car, she drove out of the parking lot and turned west toward the Lumber Jack Inn. "They're all good, but several of my sibling's K9 partners have different areas of expertise."

He nodded but didn't ask for additional information, the most people did. His expression was grim, and she understood he was preoccupied on Emily's disappearance. She didn't like knowing the cheerful nurse who'd become a good friend to Kendra was missing. The city of Cody wasn't immune to crime, but kidnapping was rather unusual. She silently prayed that this was nothing more than a misunderstanding. That Emily knew the person who'd asked for help and would be calling Doug soon.

The moment she parked in the center of the open lot, Doug pushed his door open. "I'll get things squared away inside while you and Zion work, okay?"

"Sure." She climbed out of her seat and opened the back hatch. Zion jumped down. After closing the back, she and Zion headed toward the front entrance a few paces behind Doug.

A crack of gunfire rang out. She reacted instinctively, ducking and curling her body over her K9 as Doug whirled and plastered himself against the side of the hotel, pulling his own weapon. She darted over to the building too. Thankfully, Zion came with her.

As they huddled against the side of the hotel, Maya couldn't help but wonder if the gunfire was related to Doug and Emily?

Or if her past had come back to haunt her?

www.ingramcontent.com/pod-product-compliance
Lightning Source LLC
Chambersburg PA
CBHW070417310726
48977CB00003B/725